Electronic Publishing:
Applications and Implications

Contributed papers to the
ASIS Midyear Meeting
Minneapolis, MN
May 1995

Elisabeth Logan and
Myke Gluck, editors

ASIS Monograph Series

Published for the
American Society for Information Science by

Information Today, Inc.
Medford, NJ
1997

Printed in the United States of America.

Library of Congress Cataloging-in-Publication Data

Logan, Elisabeth
    Electronic publishing : applications and implications / Elisabeth Logan
and Myke Gluck.
        p.   cm.
    Includes bibliographical references and index.
    ISBN 1-57387-036-6 (hc)
    1. Electronic publishing. I. Gluck, Myke. II. Title.
Z286.E43L64   1996
070.5'0285–dc20   96-43638
                                                                                    CIP

Price: $34.95

Published by: Information Today, Inc.
                                 143 Old Marlton Pike
                                 Medford, NJ 08055-8750

Distributed in Europe by: Learned Information Ltd.
                                 Woodside, Hinksey Hill
                                 Oxford OX1 5AU
                                 England

Book Editor: James H. Shelton
Cover Design: Jeanne Wachter

Contents

Authors and Editors: Contact Information v

1. Introduction 1
   Elisabeth Logan and Myke Gluck

   SECTION ONE: Standards and Technology Issues

2. SGML for Cultural Heritage Information 9
   Joseph A. Busch

3. Standards for Electronic Access to Geographic
   and Spatial Information 27
   Myke Gluck

4. What, If Anything, Is Cataloging
   in an Electronic World? 41
   Ling Hwey Jeng

5. Chinese Electronic Publishing on the Internet:
   Technical Approaches 55
   Huijie Chen and Hong Xu

   SECTION TWO: Electronic Publishing Applications

6. Electronic News 67
   Michael A. Shepherd, C.R. Watters, and F.J. Burkowski

7. Electronic Publishing in a University Setting:
   The Centralization vs. Decentralization Debate . . . 81
   Mary M. LaMarca

8. HortBase: An Example of Professional Societies' Roles
   in Electronic Information Systems 95
   John C. Matylonek, James L. Green,
   Evelyn Liss, and Andy Duncan

9. Access to Electronic Information:
   A Comparative Evaluation .107
   Stephen T. Bajjaly

10. Use of Book Reviews by Scholars:
   Implications for Electronic Publishing 113
   Amanda Spink and Linda Schamber

SECTION THREE: The Copyright Controversy

11. Copyright on the Internet:
   What's an Author To Do? .131
   Vicki L. Gregory and W. Stanley Gregory

Index 143

Contributing Authors and Editors

Bajjaly, Stephen T. (Chapter 9)
Assistant Professor
College of Library & Information Science
University of South Carolina
Columbia, South Carolina 29208
Tel: (803) 777-0446
Fax: (803) 777-7938
E-mail: baijaly@scarolina.edu

Burkowski, F. J. (Chapter 6)
Department of Computer Science
University of Waterloo
Waterloo, Ontario
Canada
N2L 3G1
Tel: (519) 888-4445
Fax: (519) 744-2302
E-mail: fjburkow@plg.uwaterloo.ca

Busch, Joseph A. (Chapter 2)
Program Manager
The Getty Information Institute
401 Wilshire Boulevard, Suite 1100
Santa Monica, California 90401-1455
Tel: (310) 395-1025
Fax: (310) 451-5570
E-mail: jbusch@getty.edu
http://www.getty.ahip.edu

Chen, Huijie (Chapter 5)
Reference Librarian
The Heindel Library
Pennsylvania State University Harrisburg
Middletown, Pennsylvania 17057-4898
Tel: (717) 948-6079
Fax: (717) 948-6757
E-mail: chenh@iubacs

Duncan, Andy (Chapter 8)
Associate Professor
Agricultural Communications
Oregon State University
Corvallis, Oregon 97331-4501
Tel: (541) 737-3379
E-mail: duncana@ccmail.orst.edu

Gluck, Myke, Ph.D. (Editor and Chapters 1 & 2)
Assistant Professor
School of Library and Information Studies
Florida State University
244 Shores Building
Tallahassee, Florida 32306-2048
Tel: (904) 644-8118
Fax: (904) 644-6253
E-mail: mgluck@lis.fsu.edu

Green, James L. (Chapter 8)
Professor
Department of Horticulture
Oregon State University
Corvallis, Oregon 97331-4501
Tel: (541) 737-5452
E-mail: greenjl@bcç.orst.edu

Gregory, Vicki L., Ph.D. (Chapter 11)
Assistant Professor
Division of Library and Information Science
University of South Florida
4202 East Fowler Avenue, CIS 1040
Tampa, Florida 33620-7800
Tel: (813) 974-6846
Fax: (813) 974-6840
Bitnet: dniabaa@cfrvm
Internet: gregory@luna.cas.usf.ude

Gregory, W. Stanley (Chapter 11)
Thorington & Gregory
504 South Perry Street
P.O. Drawer 1748
Montgomery, Alabama 36102
Tel: (334) 834-6222

Jeng, Ling Hwey, Ph.D. (Chapter 4)
Associate Professor
School of Library and Information Science
University of Kentucky
502 King Library South
Lexington, Kentucky 40506-0039
Tel: (606) 257-5679
E-mail: lhjeng00@ukcc.uky.edu

LaMarca, Mary M. (Chapter 7)
Assistant Director of Information Systems
Dartmouth College
6028 Kiewit
Hanover, New Hampshire 03755-3523
Tel: (603) 646-1418
Fax: (603) 646-2810
E-mail: mary.lamarca@dartmouth.edu

Liss, Evelyn (Chapter 8)
Publications Coordinator
Agricultural Communications
Oregon State University
Corvallis, Oregon 97331-4501
Tel: (541) 737-0807
E-mail: lisse@ccmail.orst.edu

Logan, Elisabeth, Ph.D. (Editor and Chapter 1)
Associate Dean
School of Library and Information Studies
Florida State University
Tallahassee, Florida 32306-2048
Tel: (904) 644-8106
E-mail: logan@lis.fsu.edu

Matylonek, John C. (Chapter 8)
Librarian and Web Coordinator
Information Services
Oregon State University
Corvallis, Oregon 97331-4501
Tel: (541) 737-7274
E-mail: matylon@ccmail.orst.edu

Schamber, Linda, Ph.D. (Chapter 10)
Assistant Professor

School of Library and Information Sciences
University of North Texas
P.O. Box 13796
Denton, Texas 76203-6796
Tel: (817) 565-2445
Fax: (817) 565-3101
E-mail: schamber@lis.unt.edu

Shepherd, Michael A. (Chapter 6)
Department of Mathematics, Statistics & Computing Science
Dalhousie University
Halifax, Nova Scotia
Canada
B3H 3J5
Tel: (902) 494-2572
Fax: (902) 494-5130
E-mail: shepherd@cs.dal.ca

Spink, Amanda, Ph.D. (Chapter 10)
Assistant Professor
School of Library and Information Sciences
University of North Texas
P.O. Box 13796
Denton, Texas 76203-6796
Tel: (817) 565-2781
Fax: (817) 565-3101
E-mail: spink@lis.unt.edu

Watters, C. R. (Chapter 6)
Jodrey School of Computer Science
Acadia University
Wolfville, Nova Scotia
Canada
B0P 1X0
Tel: (902) 542-2201, ext. 1392
Fax: (902) 542-4699
E-mail: cwatters@dragon.acadiau.ca

Xu, Hong (Chapter 5)
Graduate School of Library and Information Science
University of Illinois at Urbana Champaign
501 East Daniel Street
Champaign, Illinois 61820
e-mail: hong@alexia.lis.umiv.edu

Chapter 1

Introduction

Elisabeth Logan
Florida State University

Myke Gluck
Florida State University

Exploring the Problem

Electronic publishing is not just old wine in new bottles; it is a complex and developing arena for information provision. Few of the procedures currently in place are assured of permanence. As Internet developers, online vendors and providers, and electronic publishers explore this new and rapidly developing worldwide communications medium, unforeseen changes and adaptations are certain to follow.

Information products and delivery mechanisms have matured through many re-inventions—from clay tablets to papyrus, movable type, telegraph, telephone, radio, television, and CD-ROM. Some modes have been replaced while others have adapted to coexist in a mutually supportive information product latticework. Upscale bookstores thrive beside the CD-ROM games and the major restructuring of the entertainment, cable television, telephone, and publishing conglomerates.

The invention and deployment of networks for the development and dissemination of information, mostly in text but also in multimedia formats, raise the same concerns as did their forerunners. Questions of access, quality, and financing are three of the core overlapping issues that need to be explored in the new context of electronic media. Although these issues have been substantially resolved in regard to electronic publishing's predecessors and competitors, they still require exploration in the new setting of electronic media. Many questions may be posed in this setting: here are just a few of the many worthy of attention.

The question of access has many aspects that require immediate and long-term vigilance for electronic publishing to be equitable and stable. Is access a right or a privilege? Under our current economic system, driven by the need for capital formation from new markets and products, what information should be universally available without regard for the ability to pay or the equipment to obtain it? Is government information to be disseminated universally or only to those who can pay additional costs beyond the taxes used to generate the information? Should any, some, or all of the information content of the Internet be as universally available as telephones in the U.S.?

How do we archive and preserve the information produced, especially as the technology itself becomes obsolete? How do we ensure the fidelity of the information in electronic media? That is, how does a receiver know that the information is as the author intended?

What standards are needed to permit access and use of the information in electronic formats? Who will decide on these standards? What needs to be done to provide international access to information? What forms of cataloging and metadata are needed to provide access and to help users decide whether even to pursue electronic documents? What are reasonable roles for libraries/information centers and their employees as administration, technical services and patron interactions are transformed by and transform electronic publishing?

How will individuals, organizations, society, and social relations be affected, and how will the nature of information as process, product, resource, and commodity be transformed by the movement to electronic information? How will resources (power) be redistributed? Who will benefit and who will lose as electronic information becomes more pervasive?

How are the commercial information products to be marketed so as to provide entrepreneurs needed return on investment? What is a reasonable balance for copyright law between encouraging creativity and dissemination, and protecting revenue streams? How are esoteric products to be encouraged while maintaining a financially viable infrastructure? Are journal article authors to be compensated or paid "page" charges even in an all-electronic environment? What are the financial and logistical differences between print and electronic publishing? What information should continue to be, or might be "better" if, published on paper?

And, as one last question, how will the integration and, perhaps, eventual preponderance of electronic information come about? What are the mechanisms, forces, and players that will bring this new electronic media wine to the thirsty?

As Quinn (1995) points out, the transformation of information products from paper-based to electronic formats is necessarily constrained by current publishing practices, the credibility that printed products have because of the gatekeeping and reviewing processes they undergo, and the inertia of the traditional publishing system. Although dynamic, publishing has been an essentially stable enterprise; that is, it has found how to succeed by adapting readily to challenge and change. But the electronic frontier is a qualitative change that creates the need for a paradigmatic shift by publishers. The product is still information, but to maintain profitability as the forms and uses of information change appears to require that enterprises make more than the usual minor adjustments, including both their legal status and social views.

Perhaps one of the more troublesome aspects of the movement to electronic publishing is that books (or journals) in paper form represent an elegant and robust solution for the transmission of information in both text and graphic form. The book as medium is still unsurpassed and not easily replaced. It is highly transportable, needs no additional technology for its use, has a long shelf life, and is familiar. The current electronic delivery mechanisms (Newton, other Personal Data Assistants, and Electronic book technology notwithstanding) pale when compared to the quality of books.

Electronic delivery mechanisms do not yet have the usability or usefulness of books, although they do provide some different functionality. In particular, search and retrieval is not as precise, as rapid, or as comprehensive with a book as it can be with the application of software to electronic publications, yet users often print their results. People are comfortable with books, not because of some fetish or attachment to the past, but because of the quality solutions they provide for real people in a real world. An electronic mechanism is not about to supplant books for the millions of readers who curl up in beds or chairs or sofas to read. Different functionality has not been sufficient to overcome our rapture with books.

Speaker of the House Newt Gingrich recently drew a parallel between the change from radio to television and the nascent change from television to interactive multimedia delivery of education, entertainment, "edutainment," and "infotainment." He pointed out to an audience of high school students that their children will be amazed to learn that the interactive and user-driven television that they know was once passive and unresponsive to viewers' commands and queries. The students' children, Gingrich pointed out, will be as uncomprehending as were these students to find that their parents used to sit around a wooden box with no images and listen to radio sagas. But note that radio is still here; it is difficult to drive a car and watch television, and a radio as companion makes outdoor exercise much less boring. Radio programming has changed, yet many National Public Radio stations air reruns of 1930-50s comedies and dramas, and audio tape sales of those programs find a sizable market. The Speaker may be right about the quaintness of current technology when viewed retrospectively; however, books may outlast television as we know it.

What role can librarians and information professionals play in this march to electronic publishing? Quinn goes so far as to suggest that academic librarians become publishers, especially for esoteric journals (ibid). The basic role of librarians as intermediaries and organizers will not go away quickly. The use of Dewey, the Universal Dewey Classification, the Library of Congress Classification, and other traditional knowledge representation schemes in electronic environments, as well as new and more user driven schemes, will continue to require human support for quality in retrieval (see, for example, YAHOO's menus on the World Wide Web or the user guides developed by the Internet Public Library).

People with information needs do not have the time or experience to keep up with the vast array of resources available electronically, let alone the changes in hardware and software technology. Trained searchers will continue to be needed in a range of organizations and settings. Most of the resources searchable for a fee through Dialog are not freely available on the Internet. Electronic information will not necessarily improve the quality of the resources or the ability of humans to pursue and peruse them efficiently. The roles of reference support and information organizer will not go away. The question is not whether these tasks will be done, but rather who will do them. Will librarians as they are currently constituted in settings somewhat like today's library be involved, or will others with different labels in different settings provide these services?

Exploring the Solutions

The selections appearing in this book are taken from papers presented at the Midyear Meeting of the American Society for Information Science held in Minneapolis/St. Paul, Minnesota in May 1995. The authors explore several different aspects of electronic publishing in chapters organized into two general categories: "Standards and Technology Issues in Electronic Publishing" and "Electronic Publishing Applications." A final chapter addressing legal issues of copyright in electronic media completes the book.

Section One: Standards and Technology Issues

The first presentation, by Joseph Busch, "SGML for Cultural Heritage Information," describes the information model, document analysis methodology, and proposed linking mechanisms for building an integrated multimedia cultural heritage information database available over the Internet using WWW browsers.

The next chapter, "Standards for Electronic Access to Geographic and Spatial Information," by Myke Gluck, addresses the importance of standards for electronic access to geographic and spatial information. New federal programs and standards have the potential for providing increased access to digital spatial information for experts and the public.

Chapter 4, by Ling Hwey Jeng, "What If Anything, Is Cataloging in an Electronic World?" proposes a model for electronic cataloging that becomes an integral part of the author/editor mark-up process.

Chapter 5, by Hujie Chen and Hong Xu, "Chinese Electronic Publishing in the Future: Technical Aspects," completes this section by describing issues and proposing solutions for text encoding/decoding of Chinese language electronic publishing.

Section Two: Electronic Publishing Applications

This section begins with "Electronic News," by Michael Shepherd, C.R. Waters and F.J. Burkowski, which describes an ongoing project for the development of an electronic news delivery system incorporating newscasts and video clips with a text backbone. A full prototype of the project was demonstrated at the G7 Economic Summit in Halifax, Canada in 1995.

Next in this section is Mary LaMarca's "Electronic Publishing in a University Setting: The Centralization vs Decentralization Debate." She examines two electronic publishing cases: The Brown University CWIS and the Brown University WWW in terms of the relevance of classic organization theory to issues of centralization and decentralization.

The third chapter in this section, "HortBase: An Example of Professional Societies' Roles in Electronic Information Systems," by James L. Green, John C. Matylonek, Evelyn Liss, and Andy Duncan, proposes a peer-reviewed, synthesized, electronic information system for storage and diffusion of agricultural information. The network, HortBase, is proposed as an example of the role of professional societies in electronic information systems.

An empirical study of the usefulness of paper-based and electronic versions of the same document set is reported by Stephen Bajjaly in "Access to Electronic Information: A Comparative Evaluation." At the Center for Technology in Government at the State University of New York at Albany, the study is part of a broad examination of the costs and benefits of providing electronic access to government information.

The final chapter in this section is an empirical study by Amanda Spink and Linda Schamber, "Use of Book Reviews by Science and Technology Scholars: Implications for Electronic Publishing," which investigates the relative importance of book reviews to science and technology scholars. Of those surveyed, 28 percent had read electronic journals and only a handful had read electronic journals containing book reviews; however, 62 percent expressed an interest in electronic journals with book reviews.

Section Three: The Copyright Controversy

The final chapter, "Copyright on the Internet: What's an Author To Do?" by Gregory and Gregory, offers a stimulating discussion of a controversial topic. It comments with humor and insight on The National Information Infrastructure Task Force Working Group on Intellectual Property's Executive Summary, fair use from the library and higher education perspective, fair use from the legal perspective, proposed solutions to the fair use dilemma in an electronic environment, and copyright ownership of scholarly works.

Conclusion

Electronic publishing presents an opportunity as well as a challenge: it will be both constraining and enabling to forms of information, to the process of informing, to the users seeking to resolve information needs, and to social relations. We have no crystal ball, yet we believe this collection of papers from the 1995 ASIS Midyear Meeting contributes to the exploration of some of the issues outlined above. Needless to say, this book will not resolve any of these issues completely, but we hope that it will clarify some of them for you.

Endnote

Quinn, Frank. 1995. A Role for Librarians in Electronic Publications. *Serials Review*.21(1):27-30. Originally distributed electronically on Ejournal: EJOUR-NAL@ALBANY.bitnet. May 1994.

SECTION ONE

STANDARDS AND TECHNOLOGY ISSUES

Chapter 2

SGML for Cultural Heritage Information

Joseph A. Busch
The Getty Information Institute

Abstract

The Consortium for the Computer Interchange of Museum Information (CIMI) develops standards for the cultural heritage community to preserve museum information in digital form and make it easier to exchange. This chapter discusses the CIMI Information Model; the development of the CIMI document type definition (DTD), which uses the Standard Generalized Markup Language (SGML) to designate content from the point of view of a data model; and issues related to linking SGML information objects.

What is Cultural Heritage Information?

Cultural heritage information consists of more than beautiful paintings displayed on white walls—which is how museums are usually imagined. The real treasure troves of cultural heritage information are archives and special collections, which can also be found in most museums. There are also many free-standing cultural heritage information archives. Cultural heritage information, broadly conceived, is the information held by museums, archives, and special collections in libraries.

For example, a typical photographic archive is part of the University of London's Warburg Institute. What visitors see when they walk into such a photographic archive are the ubiquitous red, green, black, or natural cardboard archive boxes, and filing cabinets full of black-and-white photographs for study. At the Warburg, each item is filed according to a local classification system based on the principal iconographic feature of the object depicted in the photograph. Another example of a cultural heritage archive is the Witt Library at the Courtauld Institute in London, a famous repository with more than six million visual representations of works of art. Each item is filed alphabetically by artist, in boxes arranged by the country of the artist's birth. It is very difficult to access this information unless one knows the artists' names and countries of origin.[1]

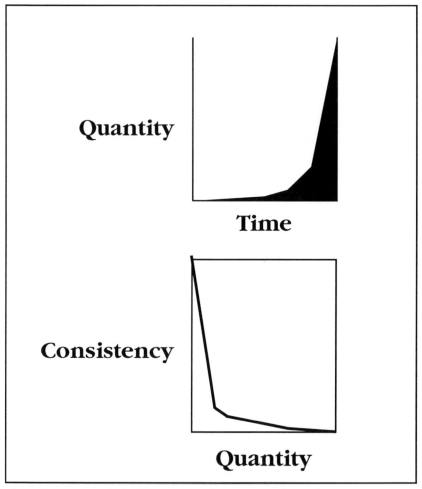

Figure 2.1a and b: Digital Information Trends in the Cultural Heritage Community

While the amount of digital information in the cultural heritage community is increasing exponentially, its consistency decreases exponentially. Figure 2.1 illustrates these trends. Until recently, much of this digital information existed in structured databases, for example, in library catalogs, museum collections management systems and, in a few cases, custom designed (i.e., idiosyncratic) retrieval systems such as those at the Warburg and the Witt. In the library community the MARC format has been in use for many years, but in the cultural heritage community no agreement on data structures or data values currently exists. In the cultural heritage community digital information currently resides in many disconnected databases located at many separate institutions, which cannot be searched coherently. Each database has different interface and command structures, and it is difficult to consolidate and analyze the results of searches.

During the past few years inexpensive personal computers have gained wide usage in the cultural heritage community. With this explosive growth, an enormous amount of relatively unstructured text (as opposed to structured databases) is being generated. Exhibition catalogs, gallery guides, wall labels, slide labels, educational materials, brochures, and finding aids are generated electronically more often than before. Although many institutions are beginning to experiment with small-scale digital imaging projects, the total number of objects being documented as digital images remain (and are likely to remain) a relatively small component of the total number of information objects generated.

Museums are more and more frequently mounting these digital files on World Wide Web sites at very low cost (but without adding much value to them other than minimal hypertext linking). Figure 2.2 illustrates the relative amounts of such digital information by various types currently and projected to the year 2000. While museums are quickly creating a public face, the problem of searching their multiple, distributed resources cannot be solved simply by putting more "stuff" up on the Web. Integrating such disparate, heterogeneous information sources is a difficult problem, but to do so is essential if this growing digital library of cultural heritage information is to be accessible in meaningful ways.

Cultural Heritage Data Standards

The cultural heritage user and vendor communities have resisted attempts to gain acceptance of the USMARC format and to develop extensions to it for the types of data attributes that this community requires, such as those needed to describe and control museum objects. This reluctance contrasts with the archives community, which developed MARC format extensions to accommodate the special attributes and functions needed to describe and control archival materials. The USMARC format for Archival and Manuscripts Control

11

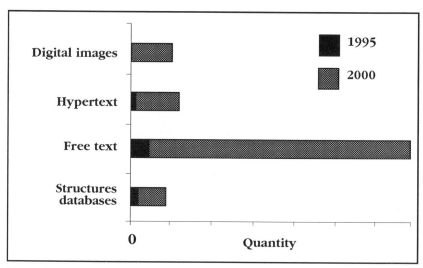

Figure 2.2: Projected Growth of Digital Information in the Cultural Heritage Community

(USMARC AMC) was developed by, and is being widely adopted and used in, the archives and manuscripts community.[2]

But in the cultural heritage community, broadly speaking, there exists no base of agreed-on information and no generally accepted standards for structuring data. Many separate databases are being developed to inventory and manage the objects in museum collections. There are many forms of museum documentation, ranging from wall labels—located on the wall next to or near the objects in a museum—which are similar to object records, to exhibition catalogs and other types of publications, which are much more sophisticated. Such published (and unpublished) documents are very complex, and include a lot of textual information broken up into discrete sections; figures, charts, and references; and often many black-and-white illustrations and color plates. To transform such a diverse set of materials into a coherent information resource—a cultural heritage database—the cultural heritage community needs to develop common ways to talk about and think about these materials.

The Consortium for the Computer
Interchange of Museum Information

The Consortium for the Computer Interchange of Museum Information (CIMI) was founded in 1990 as an operating project of the Museum Computer Network (MCN) to develop community standards, preserve digital museum information, and facilitate the exchange of information. The original CIMI project received an NEH grant to develop a standards framework (known as the CIMI Framework)[3] for interchanging digital museum information. The CIMI Framework recommended the use of several standards for encoding different types of cultural heritage information, including ISO 2709 (or MARC) and ISO 8879 (or Standard Generalized Markup Language—SGML)[4]. In 1993, the Canadian Heritage Information Network (CHIN), the Getty Art History Information Program (AHIP), and The Research Libraries Group (RLG) agreed to sponsor CIMI for three years, during which period a consortium of participating institutions would be formed and additional grant funding sought to implement projects that would demonstrate the application of the CIMI Framework.

In 1994, CIMI received a Telecommunications and Information Infrastructure Assistance Program (TIIAP) grant administered by the U.S. Department of Commerce National Telecommunications and Information Administration (NTIA); and, in 1995, a National Endowment for the Humanities (NEH) grant. The overall goal of the project, which is known as Cultural Heritage Information Online (CHIO), is to develop and demonstrate the application of standards for distributed access to heterogeneous cultural heritage information over the Internet. The CHIO project will demonstrate the application and use of SGML and the Z39.50 protocol in the cultural heritage community, and build an integrated multimedia cultural heritage information resource to demonstrate and test networked access to it.

The current CIMI consortium is a multifaceted group of institutions ranging from single museums such as the National Museum of American Art (NMAA) to consortia of archives at major European museums such as the Remote Access to Museum Archives (RAMA), a consortium of the Ashmolean, Museon, Musée d'Orsay, Prado, Pergamon, Goulandris, Museo Archeclogico Nacional, and Uffizi; to commercial organizations such as Corbis. CIMI members also include the Canadian Museum of Civilization, CHIN, Coalition for Networked Information (CNI), Eastman Kodak Company, AHIP, Museum Computer Network (MCN), Museum Documentation Association (MDA), National Gallery of Art (NGA) in Washington, D.C., Philadelphia Museum of Art, The RLG, University of California at Berkeley Museum Informatics Project, the University of California Division of Library Automation, and the Victoria & Albert Museum (V&A).

The purpose of the TIIAP-funded CHIO Structure project is to demonstrate the application and use of SGML in building an integrated multimedia cultural heritage information resource accessible over the Internet. Figure 2.3 provides an overview of the major steps in the CHIO Structure project. From July to December 1994 project working groups developed an overall information model; from January to March 1995 they collected samples of different kinds

13

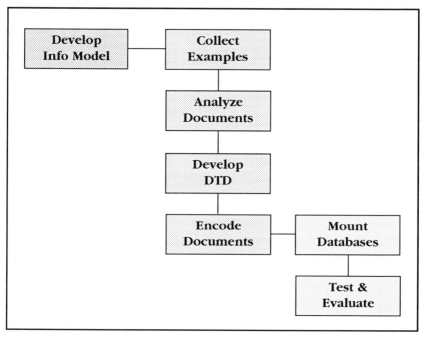

Figure 2.3:   Overview of CHIO Structure Project

of cultural heritage documentary materials; and from April to June 1995 they analyzed the structure and content of each of these "document" genres. In June and July 1995 their analysis was used as the basis for developing an SGML document type definition (DTD), and document encoding using the CIMI DTD was begun in August 1995. A database for holding SGML objects was designed and the SGML-encoded documents were mounted as a prototype in October 1995. The database was made available for public access over the Internet beginning in March 1996. Testing and evaluation of the CHIO database is ongoing. This chapter focuses on the CIMI Information Model and the process used to develop the CIMI DTD.

A Framework for Organizing Cultural Heritage Information

CIMI has taken a fresh look at the various types of cultural heritage information. It has spent considerable time developing a model for representing and organizing the information, and the model differs somewhat from the one that evolved in the bibliographic community. The CIMI model for integrating cultural heritage information is illustrated in Figure 2.4. This simplified representation of the

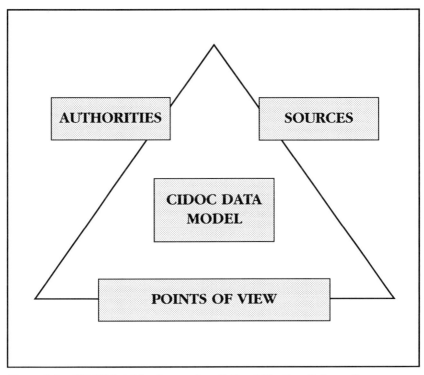

Figure 2.4: CIMI Model for Integrating Cultural Heritage Information

CIMI information model has three components: *Sources*, *Authorities*, and *Points of View*.

Sources

Sources are actual documents, both published and unpublished, as well as other materials that exist in many different genres. For example, exhibition catalogs are a genre of museum publications. Critical essays and educational materials are genres of museum publications where structure and content differ from exhibition catalogs. Genres of archival materials include sketchbooks, letters, photographs, manuscripts, etc., as well as the aids developed by archivists for finding them, or finding aids. Other genres of source materials include wall labels, collections management records, and images themselves, which may or may not have text attached to them.

Authorities

Authorities include materials that the library community has traditionally called authorities, as well as other data that has been analyzed and structured according to community data standards. Authorities are generally surrogates for source materials, but do not include all surrogates. For example, museum collections management records (or library circulation records) are not authorities because such transaction records record information related to the life cycle of an object. Collections management information is a genre of business records rather than an authority. A database that analyzes such business records, particularly across institutions and over time, might be considered an authority. This category includes traditional kinds of authorities such as authority files for personal and institutional names, geographic locations, object names, and topics as well as bibliographic databases such as abstracting and indexing services, and certain other databases that contain highly structured secondary and tertiary material. The CIMI information model recognizes that such data records have a special meaning and usefulness as pointers to sources; thus they are more tightly bound conceptually to source materials than in the library community model.

Points of View

Points of View represent the ways that users access cultural heritage information. Users may access the information through authorities that point to sources through a mediated query, or they may access the sources themselves through a full-text search. Those interested in accessing cultural heritage information also have many different intellectual points of view. A school teacher looking for classroom materials for fifth graders, a weekend museum visitor, an armchair network surfer, a museum curator, or a Ph.D. candidate working on a dissertation have very different needs and expectations from a distributed multimedia cultural heritage information resource. Project CHIO will focus on two points of view: one for art-historical, research-oriented users and one for the general public. The project will investigate how those two points of view differ and how they coincide.

Translating points of view into queries that can be processed by information servers, pointing queries to (and between) authorities and sources, and presenting a usable response to the user, require a common "glue," an interface; that is, an exhaustive data model. The Documentation Committee of the International Council of Museums (CIDOC), a UNESCO affiliate, has developed and maintains such a cultural heritage information data model (called the CIDOC Data Model)[5]. Unlike MARC, the CIDOC Data Model is an entity-relationship device. Ultimately it will be used to link the various types of resources as well as these resources to the points of view for accessing them.

In summary, the CIMI Information Model contains the following components: very structured types of information, called *Authorities*; less structured types of information that exist in various media, called *Sources*; and *Points of View* for art historians and the general public to access these information resources. Finally, the CIDOC Data Model provides an interface among these components.

The CIMI SGML Document Type Definition (DTD)

This section discusses the process for atomizing genres of source documents such as those that will be included in the CHIO Project—exhibition catalogs and wall labels. These elements need not be limited to the actual material contained in the source document, but the sources of these materials need to be considered as well. For example, an illustration may be derived from a digital image file, which in turn may be derived from a real object, such as a painting in a museum.

Figure 2.5 illustrates the major components of a *complete publication* such as an exhibition catalog. Generally, such a publication has three parts: the *front matter*, the *body*, and the *back matter*. The front matter generally consists of the title page recto and verso, table of contents, introduction, and acknowledgments. The front matter is the principal source for the bibliographic description of the overall document.[6] The bibliographic description could be enhanced to include a named location such as a Uniform Resource Locator (URL) for linking to or

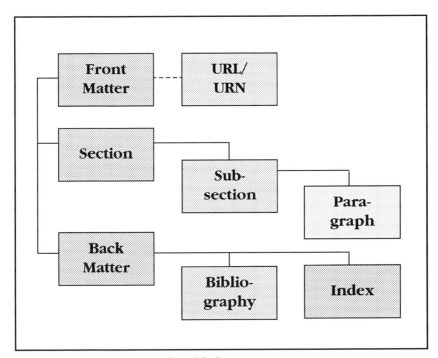

Figure 2. 5: Full Publication Item Markup

from its entire digital representation. The body of the publication contains the primary content of the document. From a structural perspective, the document body generally consists of sections, subsections, and paragraphs; it may also contain specially formatted text such as tables, as well as illustrations and other visual materials. The back matter generally contains the bibliography and index, materials that can provide additional, enhanced access to parts of the document, or links between it and other related source materials.

Figure 2.6 illustrates some of the possible components of a *paragraph* including footnotes or endnotes generally linked to the bibliography. The text may contain quotations that might have citations to their sources attached, and the citations may have a bibliographic link attached to them. The text within a paragraph may refer to several types of illustrations, which may include specially formatted text such as lists or tables. Illustrations, which also generally have captions, might be linked to external sources such as a digital image, or the data file used to generate a table or chart.

Figure 2.7 illustrates some of the various types of information or data types that might be found within the *text* of a paragraph. Encoding text can be done manually or with computer assistance. Algorithms are becoming available that

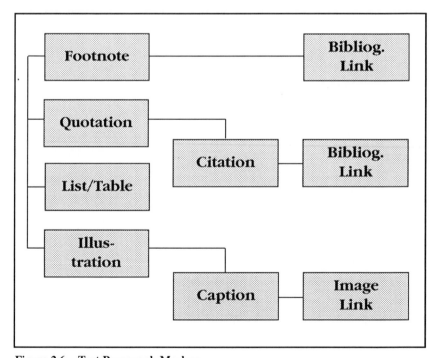

Figure 2.6: Text Paragraph Markup

can reliably identify names.[7] Not all text can be meaningfully encoded—but the more of its content that can be encoded provides more access points to that text. For example, text may contain personal and institution names, locations, topics, and dates, all of which might be identified as such.

In some cases adding information about the context of an encoded text (which may not be explicit in the text) would be useful. Using SGML, such added information can be encoded as *attributes* that surround a section, adding information such as access points to it. For example, the string "Erastus Salisbury Field," referring to a famous New England itinerant artist, may be identified within text as the general topic of that text, or it may refer to the creator of a particular work of art. Adding a role attribute to the text encoding would be helpful to distinguish between Erastus Salisbury Field as a subject and Erastus Salisbury Field as an artist/creator. It would also be useful to specify a standard form of the artist name explicitly as an artist name attribute, or to link, using a link attribute, this encoded element to a name authority file of artistic personalities, which brings together variations in spelling and format.

Encoding the context for named events by adding location, topic, and date attributes is another example of information that could be added to enhance

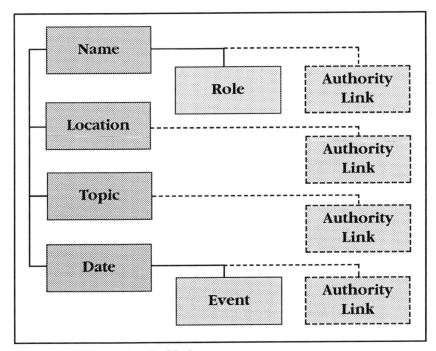

Figure 2.7: Access Points for Markup

19

access to and meaning of text. Appendix 1 is a list of attribute names, the *Categories for the Description of Works of Art*, that might be applied.[8]

Figure 2.8 illustrates the types of information a name authority generally comprises. These fields could be represented as a group of attributes to add context and consistency encoding, as discussed above. Similar attribute groups could be developed for encoding other authorities such as for locations, topics, events, or dates. There might also be attribute groupings between authorities: for example, biographical information encoded in a name authority might add attributes to make an event more explicit. A biographical event could be further encoded as a location, a date, and a role for that person. It might also be linked to a USMARC authority record or even an image such as a portrait of that person. Related events might even be linked to each other.

In summary, this section describes how a large information object such as an exhibition catalog can be divided into its explicit and implicit constituent parts. Potentially, it is possible to break a large document into many, many parts, and to add a great amount of implicit information. In practice, the level of detail of analysis of such documents will vary depending on the resources available and the purposes for encoding it. The goal of the CIMI project is to specify enough

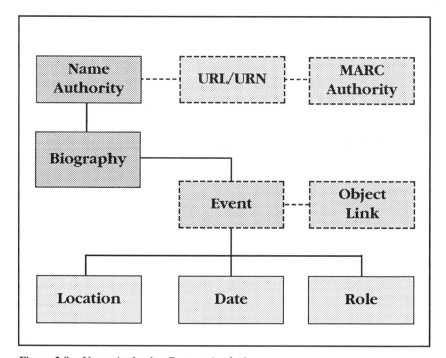

Figure 2.8:   Name Authority Content Analysis

detail, or granularity for mark-up, so that as new documents are created and existing ones re-processed, people can begin to designate the kinds of attributes that enhance access or add value to the source materials. This section also describes a methodology that can be applied to other types of information objects such as object records, wall labels, and bibliographic citations. Each genre of information will break down in somewhat different ways, but the information elements tend to converge at the level of attributes for encoding content such as names, locations, and events.

Link Naming Mechanism

Implementing the CIMI Information Model requires a robust linking mechanism to connect the parts of the distributed public information resource that it is building. The CIMI implementation must provide meaningful ways to query heterogeneously structured target databases, then present and display results from various parts of different types of sources and authorities documents.

Uniform Resource Locators, or URLs, are the way that addresses are named and accessed by the hypertext transfer protocol (HTTP) used on the World Wide Web. One of the big problems often experienced when one browses the Web is that URLs are not very robust locators and often are inadequately maintained. Generally, there is no integrity checking within the Web to ensure that URLs point to existing locations. When the name of a location that is pointed to ceases to exist temporarily or forever, or when its location or name changes, no mechanism exists to ensure that all pointers are updated. URLs are not like bar codes, physically attached to objects. Bar codes can be sequenced one for each item with controls and procedures to ensure that the same bar code identification occurs uniquely within a particular application domain for purposes such as controlling the circulation of items in a library. Nor are URLs like international standard book numbers (ISBNs) that uniquely identify publication units through a formal, community- and market-mediated process.

In an environment consisting of interconnected public resources, of which the Web is a prototype, the link naming mechanism needs to be improved with some sort of formal public identifiers (FPIs). There are two aspects to this infrastructure problem: one technical and one operational.

Implementing an FPI mechanism requires the commercial sector to develop a standard addressing protocol for encoding unique public identifiers. For example, ISBNs have been defined as a standard number of alphanumeric characters consisting of a sequence that identifies the publisher (assigned by an agreed-upon maintenance agency), a sequence assigned by the publisher, and a check digit to ensure that the sequence has a valid ISBN syntax. The maintenance agency is responsible for assigning unique identifications for publication agencies, and publication agencies are responsible for assigning identification numbers for each of their publications. FPIs might work the same way. A maintenance agency would assign unique identifications for resource publication agencies, and resource publication agencies would assign unique identifications for public servers, resources mounted on those servers, and perhaps items within those resources. The technical requirements that need to be addressed for resolving name locations down to the item level in a heterogeneous network environment are complicated, but the concept and model for such functionality are not.

From a practical perspective, implementing FPIs requires organizations that mount public information resources on servers to recognize the responsibilities that go along with providing public information resources, and to adopt operational modes that support a more robust and responsible role as publishers. On the Web, home pages come and go, and they are almost always under construction. Network-based electronic publishing on the Web and in other environments must adopt controls to ensure reliability and longevity for access to resources that are made publicly available in a formal way. For example, a model could be adopted with various levels of integrity that differentiate between formal public electronic publications such as an electronic journal, and more casual resources such as Jane Smith's home page.

Conclusion

This chapter has focused on the CIMI Information Model, document analysis methodology, and proposed linking mechanisms.[9] Implementing and accessing SGML databases present another range of technical challenges that are beyond the scope of this chapter. Briefly, the CHIO Structure project database will be accessed over the Internet using generic World Wide Web browsers. The current generation of Web client software requires either an SGML viewer or the conversion of SGML data objects to HTML. The CHIO Structure project is using SoftQuad's Panorama, a software product that converts SGML to HTML on the fly. By March 1996, the CHIO Structure project planned to have implemented multiple databases on a single server located at the Canadian Heritage Information Network that begin to demonstrate and implement the principles of the CIMI Information Model.

The second part of the CHIO project is called CHIO Access. Beginning in September 1995, CHIO Access developed a Z39.50 (ISO 10162/63) attribute set for museums, with plans to implement it on the CHIO testbed database being built as part of the CHIO Structure project. By the end of this project in March 1997, the CHIO databases will be implemented on multiple servers. By this time, CIMI plans to demonstrate interoperability with the BIB-1 attribute set, demonstrating access to cultural heritage information that is integrated with information accessed on library systems worldwide.

Endnotes

1. A full description of the Census of Antique Art and Architecture Known to the Renaissance and Witt Computer Index can be found in Joseph A. Busch, "Thinking Ambiguously: Organizing Source Materials for Historical Research." In: *Challenges in Indexing Electronic Text and Images*, Raya Fidel, Trudi Bellardo Hahn, Edie M. Rasmussen, and Philip J. Smith, eds. Medford, NJ: Learned Information, Inc., 1994.

2. See *Standards for Archival Description: a Handbook*, compiled by Victoria Irons Wallach for the Working Group on Standards for Archival Description, Chicago: The Society of American Archivists, 1994.

3. David Bearman and John Perkins, *Standards Framework for the Computer Interchange of Museum Information*, Silver Spring, MD: Museum Computer Network, May 1993. The *CIMI Framework* is available for purchase from the Museum Computer Network, 8720 Georgia Ave., Suite 501, Silver Spring, MD, 20910-3602. The *CIMI Framework* is also accessible by pointing browsers to the CIMI home page at http://www.cimi.org/cimi. Click on the Introduction icon, then click on the Publications icon, then click on the Standards Framework Document link.

4. ISO (International Organization for Standardization). ISO 8879: 1986/ A1: 1988 (E). Information Processing—Text and Office Systems—Standard Generalized Markup Language (SGML), Amendment 1. Published 1988-07-01. [Geneva]: International Organization for Standardization, 1988.

5. The CIDOC Data Model is available from the International Council of Museums Documentation Committee at http://www.icom.nrm.se/archives/ICOM/CIDOC/MODEL/Relational.Model/

6. The verso of the title page often contains a preliminary bibliographic record for the document in the form of Cataloging in Publication (CIP) data. With the increasing availability of electronic versions of documents now principally for typesetting purposes, by automatically processing a document's front matter with relatively simple algorithms the bibliographic description currently found in CIP data could be generated automatically.

7. The Berkeley Finding Aids Project (BFAP)—recently renamed Encoded Archival Description (EAD)—has developed word processing macros and Perl scripts to automatically encode personal names within text files of finding aids. Contact Daniel V. Pitti, Advanced Technologies Projects Librarian, University of California, Berkeley, 386 Library, Berkeley, California 94720, or dpitti@library.berkeley.edu for information about the Finding Aids project. The Finding Aids list server can be subscribed to at LISTSERV@library.berkeley.edu by sending the message SUB FINDAID <your name>.

8. The *Categories for the Description of Works of Art* are content guidelines developed by the Art Information Task Force (AITF), an initiative sponsored by the Getty Art History Information program (AHIP) and College Art Association (CAA). The *Categories* enhance compatibility between systems containing art information by

providing consistent access points. The *Categories* are available as a hypertext document from the Getty Art History Information program, 401 Wilshire Blvd., Suite 1100, Santa Monica, CA, 90401, or by sending a message to aitf@Getty.edu.

9. Public CIMI documents are available on the World Wide Web site. Point browsers to http://www.cimi.org/cimi to access the CIMI Web site.

Appendix 1 - Categories For the Description of Works of Art Attribute Names

OBJECT/WORK
-QUANTITY
-TYPE
-COMPONENTS
  -QUANTITY
  -TYPE
-REMARKS
-CITATIONS

CLASSIFICATION
-TERM
-SOURCE
-REMARKS
-CITATIONS

ORIENTATION/ARRANGEMENT
-DESCRIPTION
-REMARKS
-CITATIONS

TITLES OR NAMES
-TEXT
-TYPE
-DATE
-REMARKS
-CITATIONS

STATE
-IDENTIFICATION
-REMARKS
-CITATIONS

EDITION
-NUMBER OR NAME
-IMPRESSION NUMBER
-SIZE
-REMARKS
-CITATIONS

MEASUREMENTS
-DIMENSIONS
  -EXTENT
  -TYPE
  -VALUE
  -UNIT
  -QUALIFIER
  -DATE
-SHAPE
-SIZE
-SCALE
-FORMAT
-REMARKS
-CITATIONS

MATERIALS AND TECHNIQUES
-DESCRIPTION
-EXTENT
-PROCESSES OR TECHNIQUES
  -NAME
  -IMPLEMENT
-MATERIALS
  -ROLE
  -NAME
  -COLOR
  -SOURCE
  -MARKS
  -DATE
-ACTIONS
-REMARKS
-CITATIONS

FACTURE
-DESCRIPTION
-REMARKS
-CITATIONS

PHYSICAL DESCRIPTION
-PHYSICAL APPEARANCE
  -INDEXING TERMS
-REMARKS
-CITATIONS

INSCRIPTIONS/MARKS
-TRANSCRIPTION OR DESCRIPTION
-TYPE
-AUTHOR
-LOCATION
-TYPEFACE/LETTERFORM
-DATE
-REMARKS
-CITATIONS

CONDITION/EXAMINATION HISTORY
-DESCRIPTION
-TYPE
-AGENT
-DATE
-PLACE
-REMARKS
-CITATIONS

CONSERVATION/TREATMENT HISTORY
-DESCRIPTION
-TYPE
-AGENT
-DATE
-PLACE
-REMARKS
-CITATIONS

CREATION
-CREATOR
  -EXTENT
  -QUALIFIER
  -IDENTITY
    -NAMES
    -DATES/LOCATIONS
      -BIRTH
      -ACTIVE
      -DEATH
    -NATIONALITY/CULTURE/RACE
      -NATIONALITY/CITIZENSHIP
      -CULTURE
      -RACE/ETHNICITY
    -GENDER
    -LIFE ROLES
  -ROLE
  -STATEMENT
-DATE
-PLACE
-COMMISSION
  -COMMISSIONER
  -TYPE
  -DATE
  -PLACE
  -COST
-NUMBERS
-REMARKS
-CITATIONS

OWNERSHIP/COLLECTING HISTORY
-DESCRIPTION
-TRANSFER MODE
-COST OR VALUE
-OWNER
  -ROLE
-PLACE
-DATES
-OWNER'S NUMBERS
-CREDIT LINE
-REMARKS
-CITATIONS

COPYRIGHT/RESTRICTIONS
-HOLDER NAME
-PLACE
-DATE
-STATEMENT
-REMARKS
-CITATIONS

STYLES / PERIODS/ GROUPS/MOVEMENTS
-DESCRIPTION
-INDEXING TERMS
-REMARKS
-CITATIONS

SUBJECT MATTER
-DESCRIPTION
  -INDEXING TERMS
-IDENTIFICATION
  -INDEXING TERMS
-INTERPRETATION
  -INDEXING TERMS
-INTERPRETIVE HISTORY
-REMARKS
-CITATIONS

CONTEXT
-HISTORICAL/CULTURAL
  -EVENT TYPE
  -EVENT NAME
  -DATE
  -PLACE
  -AGENT
    -IDENTITY
    -ROLE
  -COST OR VALUE
-ARCHITECTURAL
  -BUILDING/SITE
    -NAME
    -PART
    -TYPE
    -PLACE
    -PLACEMENT
    -DATE
-ARCHAEOLOGICAL
  -EXCAVATION PLACE
    -SITE
    -SITE PART
    -SITE PART DATE
  -EXCAVATOR
  -EXCAVATION DATE
-REMARKS
-CITATIONS

EXHIBITION/LOAN HISTORY
-TITLE OR NAME
-CURATOR
-ORGANIZER
-SPONSOR
-VENUE
  -NAME
  -PLACE
  -TYPE
  -DATES
-OBJECT NUMBER
-REMARKS
-CITATIONS

RELATED WORKS
-RELATIONSHIP TYPE
-IDENTIFICATION
  -CREATOR
    -QUALIFIER
    -IDENTITY
      -NAMES
      -DATES/LOCATIONS
        -BIRTH
        -ACTIVE
        -DEATH
      -NATIONALITY/CULTURE/RACE
        -NATIONALITY/CITIZENSHIP
        -CULTURE
        -RACE/ETHNICITY
      -GENDER
      -LIFE ROLES
      -ROLE
  -TITLES OR NAMES
  -CREATION DATE
  -REPOSITORY NAME
  -GEOGRAPHIC LOCATION
  -REPOSITORY NUMBERS
  -OBJECT/WORK TYPE
-REMARKS
-CITATIONS

RELATED VISUAL DOCUMENTATION
-RELATIONSHIP TYPE
-IMAGE TYPE
-IMAGE MEASUREMENTS
-COLOR
-VIEW
  -INDEXING TERMS
-IMAGE OWNERSHIP
  -OWNER'S NAME
  -OWNER'S NUMBERS
-IMAGE SOURCE
  -NAME
  -NUMBER
-COPYRIGHT/RESTRICTIONS
-REMARKS
-CITATIONS

RELATED TEXTUAL REFERENCES
-IDENTIFICATION
-TYPE
-WORK CITED
-WORK ILLUSTRATED
-OBJECT/WORK NUMBER
-REMARKS

CRITICAL RESPONSES
-COMMENT
-DOCUMENT TYPE
-AUTHOR
-DATE
-CIRCUMSTANCE
-REMARKS
-CITATIONS

CATALOGUING HISTORY
-CATALOGUER NAME
-CATALOGUER INSTITUTION
-DATE
-REMARKS

CURRENT LOCATION
-REPOSITORY NAME
-GEOGRAPHIC LOCATION
-REPOSITORY NUMBERS
-REMARKS
-CITATIONS

25

Chapter 3

STANDARDS FOR ELECTRONIC ACCESS TO GEOGRAPHIC AND SPATIAL INFORMATION

Myke Gluck
Florida State University

Abstract

Cartographic and spatial information products are difficult to access in electronic and networked environments. Three major issues relevant to that access are their location, selection, and viewing. Now, new federal programs and standards may improve this situation. The United States Geological Survey (USGS) and other federal agencies under the guidance of the Federal Geographic Data Committee (FGDC) have developed certain federally mandated standards: a cataloging standard for digital spatial information (digital spatial metadata) and standards for transferring spatial information (SDTS and VPF). The USGS has also supported the proposal for a Government Information Locator Service (GILS) and for a National Geospatial Data Clearinghouse (NGDC).

The metadata standard has the potential to improve the selection of datasets by providing improved expressions for quality, accuracy, and availability. The transfer standards have the potential to provide a lingua franca for digital spatial data that will improve viewing and manipulation of spatial data. GILS has the potential to improve locating and accessing highly distributed datasets. The quantity, quality control, and application logistics of the GILS program and these standards to actually improve access for the full range of users is not yet clear. This chapter briefly describes these standards and their potential for providing increased access to digital spatial information for experts and the general public.

Introduction and Background

Geographic and spatial information permeates our information needs and resources. Often it is so well integrated into the general resources that we are not aware that the information is spatial in nature. For example, tourist information, such as airline flight times and automobile travel times, weather information, and demographic information from a census, are spatially rich information resources that we often use without noting their geographic nature.

Spatial information addresses three key user queries: What's there? Where's that? and How are this and that physically connected? Unfortunately, specific geospatial information may be difficult to select, locate, retrieve, or use. It has been estimated that 80 percent of all information produced is spatial in nature, and much of that spatial information is produced by state and local governments (Huxhold 1991). Citizens have a right to see these government generated materials; however, physical and/or intellectual access to these government sources may be extremely limited in spite of various open records laws and the Freedom of Information Act (FOIA).

Compounding the existing access problems are the exponentially growing amounts of geospatial data. The advent of digital spatial information formats and complex telecommunication and computing environments for creating and manipulating them have led to massive increases in geospatial data production. For example, NASA's missions and NOAA's weather satellites produce terabytes of information monthly, and the 1990 US Census is available on approximately a hundred CD-ROMs!

Preeminent among technological changes effecting geospatial information is the development of Geographic Information Systems (GIS). These are designed to collect, store, retrieve, transform, analyze, and display spatial information concerning objects from the real world (Burrough, 1986). Such systems describe the objects by their position, recognize spatial interrelationships indicating how places are linked, and manage attribute information from the objects that are nonspatial such as color, cost, and size. Many such GIS systems are used every day throughout the world and success stories abound. GIS has and continues to provide exciting opportunities for better analysis and management of spatial information.

Unfortunately, the use of GIS systems requires extensive training and the different systems often are not able to share data. Thus, GIS currently heightens the access barriers to digital geospatial information for a range of expert to novice users (Medyckyj-Scott and Davies 1993). Novice users include experts in other fields who lack experience in using GIS as well as casual users of digital geospatial information.

The federal government, guided by extensive user and other stakeholder organizations, has begun to move on three fronts to help reduce the access barriers to spatial information. Presidential Executive Order and public law relating to Federal Information Processing Standards (FIPS) have been the mechanisms for placing these standards into the day-to-day activities of the federal government. All of these initiatives involve standards: one addresses how digital spatial information is to be described (the metadata standard); a second addresses a service for locating, accessing and acquiring information; the third addresses the transfer or exchange of digital geospatial data among users and GIS systems.

The metadata and exchange initiatives are outgrowths of working groups from the Federal Geographic Data Committee (FGDC) composed of representatives of fourteen federal government departments and independent agencies, including the Library of Congress, concerned with geospatial data as well as others that participate on working groups and subcommittees. The locator service initiative is broader than geospatial information and addresses citizen access to government information. The locator service is called the Government Information Locator Service (GILS). The U.S Geological Survey (USGS) is also a major force in GILS developments in conjunction with the Office of Manpower and Budget (OMB) of the U.S. federal government. Although these initiatives only directly effect the federal government they will influence how spatial data is managed in both local government and private industry.

The remainder of this chapter presents these major access problems in more detail and then describes these three new federal government initiatives that may lower these access barriers.

Some Cartographic and Geospatial Information Access Barriers

Our analysis focuses on major intellectual and technical barriers to the access and use of currently available geospatial datasets. Selecting and locating, as well as retrieval, viewing, and use of spatial data are significant intellectual and technological barriers for a range of users of geospatial information. The information we address here are the datasets created with GIS or automated cartographic software and bitmapped datasets of spatial data generally formed by digitally scanning a paper or mylar map. Other factors, of course, impede access to geospatial information such as cost, production of relevant information sources for particular needs, and legal rights to access. These additional barriers are driven more by political and market forces than intellectual and technical concerns. Also, we do not discuss here other spatial information resources in traditional text and other formats. We concede that additional geospatial data, resources, and structures need to be developed; however, we restrict this discussion to the readily available datasets that currently exist or are in development.

29

Locating

Locating existing digital geospatial datasets is difficult. Attempts to support federal document locating include the *Manual of Federal Geographic Data Products* (FGDC 1992a). This Manual is a catalog for spatial products and includes both digital and more traditional formats for data such as paper and microform. It is available in print and on the Internet at http://info.er.usgs. gov/fgdccatalog/title.html. The Manual includes ordering information for a particular product.

In addition, extensive Internet-based lists are available at many sites through use of the various Internet information retrieval mechanisms (e.g., gopher, lynx, mosaic, amadeus). These lists consist of pointers to other sites as well as to particular datasets produced by private and public entities. For example, the State of Montana site lists datasets from many of its agencies at http://nris.msl.gov/gis/mtmaps.html, and Delorme, Inc. provides access to thumbnails of several of its products and points to other maps and spatial information or surrogate information sites, at http://www.delorme.com/maps/mapurls.htm. Similarly, an entry to Canadian geographic resources may be found at http://www-nais.ccm.emr.ca/.

The FGDC through the National Geospatial Data Clearinghouse (NGDC) in this country has embarked on a major project to develop a clearinghouse for distributed digital spatial information. Also, occasionally, cartographic or spatial information is subsumed under the intellectual domain of more general information needs with formats not made explicit. We make no attempt here to describe all paper, World Wide Web, or other electronic sites for spatial information. The point is that many Internet sites with spatial and digital spatial information, or their surrogates, exist. Nonetheless, no exhaustive or truly well organized method has been devised for discovering whether spatial information exists for a particular region, time period, or user task.

Several interesting user interface tools are available on the Internet to assist in locating spatial datasets. In particular, there are tools that allow a user to discern whether a site has spatial data relevant to one's needs. The use of a map overlaid with a grid is one of these tools. The user selects a cell of the grid and the system retrieves any datasets it has that include the selected map region. A modification of this tool allows the user to construct a bounding rectangle for a region on the map and the system retrieves a list of its relevant datasets. Unfortunately, these tools are crude and often difficult to employ for highly refined searches or for specific purposes.

Selecting

As just described, finding digital spatial datasets to aid in resolving an information need is difficult, if not impossible, in many situations. Similarly, the task of deciding whether one or more of the available datasets will effectively serve the user's needs is problematic; that is, selecting a dataset is also fraught with ambiguity. Its selection depends upon several factors that work together to determine the appropriateness of a particular dataset for a particular need. Among the major requirements are that the dataset cover the relevant geographical area, the appropriate attributes be described, and the quality and accuracy of both the geography and attributes meet the user's needs.

Just as a map is a representation of the earth, digital geospatial information provides a representation, albeit a simplification, of the earth and its objects. Therefore, the selection of a particular representation for a particular task has always been problematic and not made easier by automation. Improper scale of a paper map, accuracy of placement, and the projection or ellipsoid used may invalidate an otherwise useful map that covers the required region and discusses the important attributes. Also, the method of data collection and techniques of data analysis have the potential to invalidate an otherwise apparently useful map. For the user to make an informed choice, the dataset's attribute data dictionary must also be available.

The situation has not changed with digital formats and, perhaps, has worsened. For example, computer software allows the user to zoom in on a graphic. With spatial information the user may zoom in beyond the proper resolution of the spatial data and, thus, may be led to believe that no objects are there when, in truth, there are objects on the ground. The problem of cartographic generalization is a major research area within geography that computer methods have not yet resolved (Buttonfield and McMaster 1991).

Understanding the quality and accuracy of digital spatial data requires knowledge of how the data was collected, manipulated, and stored in a GIS. Current library cataloging methods (AACR2/MARC format) address some of the basic properties of digital spatial data, but they have no mechanism for systematically describing quality and accuracy, and they lack the data dictionary of digital spatial data necessary for the proper selection of a dataset.

Retrieval of Digital Spatial Information and its Use

Even when a digital spatial dataset is located and selected because of appropriate coverage and quality of attributes, the users have no guarantee that they will be able to use the dataset. More than one hundred different major GIS products are on the market, many with incompatible data formats. Consequently, a dataset produced using one product may not be usable in the user's GIS. The lack of easy transfer or exchange of digital spatial information has severely limited the use and interchange of spatial information between the public and private sectors as well as within public agencies. It is not unusual for

31

different state agencies within the same state to use different, incompatible GIS software, or for cities within the same county to use different GIS products.

For example, as stated earlier, much of Montana's major datasets are available on the Internet; yet, if a researcher did not use a compatible GIS the data would be of little value. The potential users may not be able to view the data or access the attribute descriptions. This is especially true when the underlying database managers of the GIS products are also difficult to exchange.

Spatial data is expensive to collect. Between 45 and 80 percent of the cost of a new GIS project for a jurisdiction requiring creation of a base map lies in data collection and digitization (Huxhold 1991, 243). These costs are lower for new projects that merely add layers of information onto the base map, but even here data collection costs account for approximately half of a project's total expenditures. The inability to share such expensive data among different GIS systems has impacted their more widespread cooperative use and the distribution of analyses such systems permit.

Federal Standards and Program Initiatives

A major force behind several of the initiatives of the federal government to alleviate these barriers to access for spatial data is the Federal Geographic Data Committee (FGDC). One of the FGDC's major responsibilities is "to promote the coordinated development, use, sharing, and dissemination of surveying, mapping, and related spatial data." (FGDC 1994a, 1994b) Under that responsibility the FGDC has promoted the development of a National Spatial Data Infrastructure (Executive Office . . . 1990). The NSDI is primarily directed towards creating practical digital libraries and a clearinghouse for spatial data for the federal government and other users including the states, academia, and the commercial sector. The NSDI was itself created by Executive Order 12906, signed by President Clinton on April 11, 1994.

The federal government has begun a series of initiatives to address the shortcomings detailed above. One major program of the FGDC has been the establishment of a metadata (data about data) standard. This standard requires all federally developed spatial digital datasets to be accompanied by extensive descriptions of the producers and maintainers, contents, quality, and accuracy of the dataset. The FGDC approved this new dataset description standard, called the "Content Standards for Digital Geospatial Metadata," on June 8, 1994. Paragraph B of Executive Order 12906 required all federal agencies to use the new standard for describing (cataloging) all spatial datasets produced after January 11, 1995. All agencies must also have developed a plan by April 1, 1995 to retrospectively describe to the extent practical previously developed materials. The agencies are also to make available these metadata descriptions

32

in electronic form and place them into the NSDI Clearinghouse, designed to be a distributed digital geospatial library providing the kernel of a one-stop facility to locate and access digital geospatial data. The FGDC has been funding organizations to begin the construction of this digital library infrastructure.

The second major initiative supported by FGDC members is the Government Information Locator Service (GILS) project (McClure, Ryan, and Moen 1992; McClure and Moen 1994). GILS has been motivated by sections of OMB Circular-130. GILS provides for agencies to develop records that will be placed on the National Information Infrastructure and that are practical for private citizens and businesses to identify locate, access, and acquire federal government information products. The GILS records and transfers are based upon Z39.50, the ANSI standard for Information Retrieval. GILS is a voluntary standard of the sort promoted by the OMB in Circular A-119. GILS is not specifically designed for spatial information but spatial information is included in the GILS profile.

A third initiative is a Federal Information Processing Standard (FIPS 173). FIPS 173 provides and mandates a transfer standard for digital spatial information. The standard took effect in February 1993 as voluntary and became mandatory in February 1994. It requires that federal agencies produce datasets amenable to the transfer format; that is, Requests for Proposals (RFPs) for spatial data acquisition by the federal government require that the deliverables comply with the standard. However, no exclusivity pertains because the data may be delivered in other formats, and there is no mandate to use the standard once delivered. The civilian agency standard is called the Spatial Data Transfer Standard (SDTS). A related but distinct standard exists for use by the military agencies called the Vector Product Format (VPF). Each of these exchange standards are extensive and not many translators between systems currently conform to these standards.

Metadata Standard

The spatial metadata standard has seven main sections and three supporting sections. The seven main sections cover the areas outlined as follows:

Section 1: Identification information includes information to reference the dataset, to describe the basic character of the dataset and its intended use and limitations, and to specify the time period that corresponds to ground "truth." Section One also includes status, maintenance, and update information, and describes the areal domain covered by the dataset. It lists keywords applicable to the data and the thesaurus used (if any), indicates the contact person for the dataset, describes data security issues, and lists the native software and hardware environment and filenames needed to work with the dataset.

Section 2: Data quality information includes attribute accuracy, logical consistency, completeness, positional accuracy, history of the development of the dataset (called the lineage), and the degree of cloud cover. Several of these data accuracy issues appear again in the SDTS standard described below.

Section 3: Spatial data organization includes indirect reference (names of geographic features) and direct reference methods (e.g., vector, point, or raster), and types and numbers of spatial objects, whether vector, point, or raster.

Section 4: Spatial reference information refers to data such as horizontal and vertical coordinates, ellipsoid, and projection.

Section 5: Entity and attribute information includes the description of the content of the dataset, accuracy of attributes, and the domain from which data attributes may be assigned; that is, a data dictionary.

Section 6: Distributor information describes ordering information.

Section 7: Provides information on the currency of the metadata and the person responsible for maintaining the metadata.

The three supporting sections describe how to encode the citation information, how to describe the time period information, and how to present the contact information. These support sections do not stand alone but are embedded in the proper sections of the major divisions.

It should be obvious that this spatial metadata is much more detailed than current AACR2 cartographic information cataloging standards. The information is much more extensive in the areas of accuracy and quality of both the topological and nontopological data, and in the details of who maintains the dataset and who maintains the metadata for the dataset. Also, these metadata include the history of the development of the dataset (lineage). GIS experts need much of this data to decide on the legitimacy of a given dataset for an intended purpose. Often data may cover the appropriate time and place and offer a useful projection, but prove inappropriate because of the accuracy or quality of either the topological or non-topological attributes.

From a general or casual user's perspective the metadata, indeed, is overkill. It is important to note that the standard does not address the display of the information. Thus, a general purpose user faces a daunting task in evaluating all the information in the metadata in order to decide on its appropriateness for a particular task, such as checking on the floodplain near her/his home or in getting travel information. Much work must be spent in designing high fidelity displays of metadata and attributes that minimize user misuse and, yet, effectively inform general or casual users.

The role of traditional library systems to display the new spatial metadata and how the metadata standard may effectively interact with traditional library cataloging to aid resolution of a casual user's information needs is not yet clear. Also, our experience indicates that even experienced catalogers will need extensive training to implement this metadata standard (Jue et al. 1994). The spatial information community is rightly concerned with having sufficient dataset description to avoid misuse of information; however, spatial metadata must also be usable and useful for the full range of users.

Government Information Locator Services (GILS)

A locator is defined as an information resource that identifies other information resources, describes the information available in those resources, and provides assistance in how to obtain the information. GILS is an effort to facilitate locating, accessing, and acquiring publicly available U.S. federal government information resources. A major impetus to this initiative is the development of the National Information Infrastructure (Clinton and Gore 1993) and the increasing amount of federal resources in electronic formats. On June 25, 1993, the Office of Management and Budget (OMB) revised Circular A-130 (58 F.R. 36068, July 2, 1993), "Management of Federal Information Resources," to better manage government information and provide for more user support. Circular A-130 encourages agencies to employ new technologies in a timely and fair manner using an array of public and private sources. The GILS is a mandatory program for agencies driven by A-130, the Records Disposal Act (Title 44 of the United States Code) as well as the Freedom of Information Act (FOIA). GILS uses voluntary standards and is not restricted to spatial or electronic information alone. Further guidance is outlined for implementating GILS by agencies in the *Paperwork Reduction Act (PRA) of 1995* (PL104-13). The PRA amends 44 USC Chapter 35 effective October 1, 1995. Section 3506d of the PRA codifies Circular A-130 from OMB providing guidance in dissemination of records showing concern for users, costs, and critical restraints.

The USGS has been a major supporter of the program, including the funding for the development of an application profile for network-based GILS implementations that references the Z39.50 as well as other standards for use in the National Information Infrastructure. This GILS Profile is under review by the National Institute for Standards and Technology (NIST) and will become Federal Information Processing Standard (FIPS) 192. The Office of Manpower and Budget (OMB) has issued a bulletin, entitled "Establishment of Government Information Locator Service," which describes the government-wide policy framework for GILS and references the profile for GILS described in FIPS 192 (OMB 1995). The OMB Bulletin applies to all departments and agencies in the Executive Branch and requests that independent regulatory commissions and agencies comply. The GILS implementation will be phased in over the next few years.

GILS users will access the information both directly themselves and indirectly through intermediaries. Direct online access through the Internet is, of course, envisioned as is access by 800 numbers, fax, and almost any possible delivery route.

Another component of GILS will use network technology to support many different data views from separate locators. GILS organizes a decentralized, agency-based group of locators and information services. Decentralization permits the responsibilities for support and maintenance of the information to be close to those who understand the information and who directly serve each agency's primary users.

Among the GILS set of locator records are those identified by agencies as belonging to the GILS Core. The GILS Core is defined as the set of records that will comply with the defined GILS Core Element standards, that will be mutually accessible through interconnected electronic network facilities, and that will be provided without charge to the direct user. Each agency will maintain its own records in the GILS Core. The GILS Core is projected to contain no more than 100,000 locator records, including no more than 1000 locator records for information systems records for each federal agency that is a major disseminator of public information (fewer for agencies that are not major disseminators). Most information sources accessible to GILS direct users would not be considered part of the GILS Core, and fees may be charged for those records not maintained by the federal government.

Content definitions describe the GILS Core Elements, relations within and between GILS Core Elements, and GILS relations to the USMARC format for bibliographic data. Users employ these elements to determine the relevance of defined information resources for their needs and to learn how to obtain the information resources. ANSI Z39.50 definitions for GILS Core Elements in a GILS Profile serve as a structure and format for transfer of the GILS Core Elements between computer systems. A GILS profile is intended for English language users but it is also designed to be extensible to other languages. For spatial data, GILS will also include several elements in common with the Spatial Data Transfer Standard (SDTS) data exchange standard and the metadata standard. Also, the GILS profile's initial modifications are to change current wording and instead use SDTS vocabulary for spatial element names.

There is also an international movement afoot to create a global GILS joining information from many countries. The push for a GGILS has come from the G-7 economic powers.

Spatial Data Exchange Standards

Since February 1994 the availability of a standard format for spatial data transfer or exchange has been required for all new datasets procured by all federal agencies. An exchange standard presents a set of rules for structuring the information so that a sender can deliver unambiguous data to a receiver

(Kottman 1992). It is similar to Morse code, ASCII, and EBCDIC encodings that permit high fidelity between character data sent and character data received. Unfortunately, spatial data is much more complex than mere character data. An effective exchange requires that many issues—physical characteristics of the transport media (e.g., CD-ROM, tape), what features are of mutual interest, logical organization of the information and its structure, definitions for features and attributes, descriptions of the instances and types of features and attributes, directory structure for multiple file transfers, and metadata agreements as well as information on the tools used for compiling, displaying, and data manipulations—must all be agreed upon and understood by both the sender and receiver. Software that converts one spatial data format to another using the standard and the dataset's metadata is the mechanism for the exchange of spatial data between different systems and formats. Unfortunately, separate converters will be needed for each distinct format to provide the exchange.

Actually two federal standards are in use at this time: the Vector Product Format (VPF; MIL-STD 600006), used by the military, is a subset of the more general DIGEST format standard; civilian agencies use the Spatial Data Transfer Standard (SDTS; FIPS 173) or its subset, the Topological Vector Profile (TVP) used by USGS and the U.S. Census Bureau. Three major differences between these two standards are that the SDTS uses ISO 8211 encapsulation while VPF uses custom headers on the physical medium, SDTS/TVP uses an object model for the logical schema built around real world features and their attributes while VPF data is based on relational tables, and VPF expects direct use in the field for particular tasks and not just the exchange of data for general purposes as SDTS/TVP (Hogan 1995). Encapsulation refers to the scheme used to structure files, blocks, records, and fields on the media. Even with the complexity of the current mandated standards not all areas of agreement between receiver and sender are fully implemented (i.e., user interface and receiver tools).

Each of these exchange standards provides for the transfer of files, records, fields, and subfields with the following objectives as described in SDTS documentation (FGDC,1992b):

    a) to encode in a standard format;

    b) to provide for machine and media independence;

    c) to accompany the data with their description;

    d) to preserve all meaning and relationships of the data; and

    e) to keep both field and records to an appropriate maximum length.

Two major difficulties surface in developing the SDTS standard. First, it is a general standard much like Standard Generalized Markup Language (SGML), which gives developers much latitude in its implementations; second, there is great variety in attribute definitions and values among various data dictionaries (Hogan 1995).

The USGS has begun to provide SDTS compliant data if requested by users. It has also decided to place some datasets (1:1.2 Million DLGs) free on the Internet in SDTS format while other formats for the same data will be provided to users for a fee (ibid).

Kottman (1992) points out eight additional aspects of spatial data exchange that must be addressed to move further towards making the process of exchange of spatial data as transparent as the exchange of spreadsheet data:

- attention to version control and to tracking short transactions on the data,
- better support for very large databases (many spatial datasets are considered very large databases and need special handling),
- better integration for raster, vector, text, and other data types for transport,
- improved ease and transparency of processing and translation,
- improved data quality management to assist in metadata generation and its interpretation,
- better security in GIS environments both for national security and personal privacy,
- better thesaurus control for data dictionaries to improve conversion from one dictionary to another, and
- improved metadata location and access for datasets that are public or commercially available which meet transfer standards.

Much has been gained by this start towards spatial data exchange standards, including the meeting of consumers and producers to better understand each others' needs. The first major versions of standards for spatial data exchange are accepted and in place, but they are not yet fully functional nor are they yet meeting the needs of the user community. Driven by the requirements of producers and consumers, the standards process will surely move over time to better meet those needs.

Conclusions

Each of these standard processes has initiated making digital spatial data more accessible both intellectually and physically. Such access is a very complex issue with many stakeholders carrying various agendas. The spatial data standards' stakeholders are struggling to find common ground among producers and consumers, private and government groups, and expert and casual user communities. This is no easy task, but a strong basis in the standards process has begun. The synergy of these three federal standards (GILS, SDTS, and Metadata) is encouraging; each adds a piece to the goal of making easy and transparent the user processes of locating, selecting, obtaining, and using spatial data.

Again, these issues at the federal level are slowly being addressed. Nonetheless, much of the spatial data is being developed on the state and local level where these standards are not mandatory and often may be in conflict with local needs and traditions. The states are discussing these issues, too; however, nationwide standards are not yet in sight. As the federal standards mature and are more responsive to producers and consumers, the need for conformity and the ease of future use may well overcome much of the current reticence on the state and local level to adopt federal standards or their future versions as their own.

In closing, the future of these standards and the benefits to be derived from them may well be in jeopardy in spite of recent federal support. The climate in Washington is changing and the drive to facilitate these standards developments may wane as Congress limits federal regulations and/or cuts spending. For example, there have been serious discussions concerning the future existence of the USGS, which continues to play a significant role in these initiatives for improved intellectual and physical access. All stakeholders endorse the information superhighway, and these standards may be seen as part of the life support for making the national information infrastructure responsive to users' geospatial information needs. Continued support and funding for these standards will further lower access barriers, enabling users to better resolve their growing spatial information needs. Thus, these standards separately and collectively promote Jeffersonian democracy through access to information. We hope the Congress's support for spatial information access will continue in spite of the drive to reduce federal spending.

References

Burrough, P. A. 1986. *Principles of Geographic Information Systems for Land Resources Assessment.* Oxford University Press.

Buttonfield, B. and R. McMaster, eds. 1991. *Map Generalization: Making Rules for Knowledge Representation.* Longman.

Clinton, President William J. and Vice President Albert Gore, Jr. 1993. *Technology for America's Strength, A New Direction to Build Economic Strength.* Washington: Government Printing Office. February 22.

Executive Office of the President. Office of Management and Budget. 1990. Revised Circular A-16. *Coordination of Surveying, Mapping, and Related Spatial Data Activities.* October 19.

Federal Geographic Data Committee. 1994a. *Content Standards for Digital Geospatial Metadata.* June 8.

Federal Geographic Data Committee. 1994b. *Content Standards for Digital Geospatial Metadata Workbook*. Draft December 1; version 0.5). Washington: Federal Geographic Data Committee.

Federal Geographic Data Committee. 1992a. *Manual of Federal Geographic Data Products*. Office of Information Resources Management. U.S. Environmental Protection Agency. Prepared for EPA under contract 68-W90065. Falls Church, VA: Vigyan.

Federal Geographic Data Committee. 1992b. *A Prototype SDTS Federal Profile for Geographic Vector Data with Topology* (Draft: 02-14-92). Washington: Federal Geographic Data Committee.

Hogan, Richard. 1995. Personal communication. [Describes the current implementation status of the SDTS, its relation to VPF, and future use of the standards.]

Huxhold, W. 1991. *An Introduction to Urban Geographic Information Systems*. New York: Oxford University Press.

Jue, D., D. Stage, M. Gluck, C. Koontz, and C. Kacmar. 1994. *The Integration of Citizens and State and Local Governments into the National Spatial Data Infrastructure Initiatives*. Proposal to the U.S. Department of Commerce/USGS. Funded Project in Progress.

Kottman, C. A. 1992. *Some Questions and Answers about Digital Geographic Information Exchange Standards, 2nd ed*. Intergraph Corporation.

Medyckyj-Scott, D. and C. Davies. 1994. Personal communication. [Describes their survey results of users of geographic information systems conducted in the United Kingdom.]

McClure, Charles R. and William E. Moen. 1994. *Expanding Research and Development on the ANSI/NISO Z39.50 Search and Retrieval Standard (Final Report)*. Syracuse, NY: School of Information Studies, Syracuse University.

McClure, Charles R., Joe Ryan, and William E. Moen. 1992. *Identifying and Describing Federal Information Inventory/Locator Systems: Design for Networked-based Locators*, 2 Vols. Bethesda, MD: National Audio Visual Center

Office of Manpower and Budget. 1995. *Establishment of Government Information Locator Service*. OMB 95-01. Federal Register, December 7, 1994, Vol. 59234, pp. 63075-77.

Chapter 4

What, If Anything, Is Cataloging in an Electronic World?

Ling Hwey Jeng
University of Kentucky

Abstract

The concept of the library of the future has been discussed extensively during the last decade. Current development of the Internet resources is one step toward that direction, however, the methods of organizing Internet resources appear to be far from ideal. We begin this chapter with a description of what has been known as library cataloging, and proceed with a review of current attempts to organize electronic information objects. Then, we discuss some issues related to current practice in organizing electronic resources, and we conclude with our proposal for a model of what cataloging should be in the electronic world and suggest what needs to be done to realize this model.

Introduction

In her *Analytical Review of the Library of the Future*, Drabenstott (1994) collected twelve different definitions of the library of the future offered by scholars in our field. Although the library of the future is called under many different names—"electronic library," "virtual library," "digital library," "bionic library," "library without walls"—the definitions share many common characteristics. This future library will emphasize user access to information rather than ownership of materials. The option of instant information delivery through direct links to remote files is assumed. The future library uses the maximum power of available electronic technology, and constantly updates its records and offers its users intelligent services. In this future library, access is done in absence of time and place constraints. The library's collection reflects true integration of traditional materials and electronic resources. We propose a good definition of the library of the future as a system that utilizes the maximum power of technology to link cataloging and indexing as well as primary and textual databases into an online network, the purpose of which is to provide users universal access to locally owned and remotely available information sources.

The key in this concept of the future library is "electronic text." In an electronic world, organization occurs in whatever way needed to provide quick and thorough access to information regardless of its physical constraint, or lack of it. One way to better understand the nature of organization in this future library is to take a chronological approach to library cataloging, as we do in the next section of this chapter.

The Characteristics of Traditional Cataloging

Ample literature exists on the description, principles and practice of traditional cataloging, which need not be repeated here. A cursory look at the definition of a catalog reveals some of the characteristics of the traditional practice of cataloging. The American Library Association, in its *Anglo-American Cataloging Rules* (Gorman and Winkler 1988), defines a catalog as: "(1) A list of library materials contained in a collection, a library, or a group of libraries, arranged according to some definite plan. (2) A list of materials prepared for a particular purpose (e.g. an exhibition catalog, a sales catalog)."

These two definitions show that traditional cataloging is based on physical formats. It assumes homogeneous collections, and is primarily location bound. The emphasis in practice is on a uniform approach to organization and arrangement. Traditional catalogs serve the purposes of known item search, category search, and choice of entries, as Cutter spelled out originally in 1876 (Cutter, 1904). These purposes are met through bibliographically significant access points such as authors, titles, and subject headings, in addition to some commonly used alphanumeric search keys, such as ISBN. An alternative is to use a subject approach to access within certain hierarchical structures, such as a classification system. The indexing files for traditional catalogs are quite predictable. Library bibliographic databases use inverted file structures with linear order in their arrangement.

Most of these characteristics, however suitable for the traditional world of bibliographic resources, do not apply as well to the organization of an electronic world. A great distance separates the traditional resources and the electronic resources in current practice of cataloging. As Erik Jul (1995a) points out on the INTERCAT listserv: "Books and similar things benefited from bibliographic description and access; Internet resources did not. Books and similar things could be located using the library catalog; Internet resources could not. . . . Two worlds arose: the library and its catalog and the Internet and its current, most favorite searching/browsing/grazing/burrowing scheme."

By no means, however, do we suggest that catalogers remain isolated, unaware of the development of electronic technology and the changes in the library landscape. On the contrary, especially those in academic libraries, catalogers were one of the first to embrace the Internet technology as part of their work routines. Through bibliographic utilities like OCLC and RLIN, network systems like Internet, and organizations such as LC, catalogers have been actively engaged in e-mail exchanges related to their jobs, and participated in one of the largest electronic listservs, AUTOCAT. Cataloging records in MARC format have been made available via Internet by several institutions, including Australian Bibliographic Network, Library of Congress MARC records distribution, and RLIN, which allow export of MARC records to a file transfer protocol (ftp) file.

Catalogers have also taken advantages of Internet resources such as World Wide Web to enhance their work. The Web allows them quick access to a library, and it provides answers to questions related to foreign language material. The Web is a useful tool when foreign language experts in other institutions need to be located quickly for their expertise. Also, the Web is excellent as a reference source for new subject/topical areas when catalogers see the need for familiarizing themselves with new subjects. And finally, as Stewart (1995) points out, the majority of cataloging tools are now updated in electronic format available on Internet URL sites (e.g., LC Marvel, LC ftp, OCLC ftp).

Catalogers cannot ignore Internet resources without depriving themselves of opportunities for professional enhancement. But what most catalogers did not realize are the opportunities the Internet provides to shape the making and evolution of the electronic world from the start, and to take the lead in terms of developing how the Internet resources can be structured to help the process of organization.

Current Status of Organization in the Electronic World

The electronic world is messy, volatile, and uncontrolled. Consider the multiple versions of an electronic information object, for example. The electronic text could be made available in standalone plain ASCII file, or a standalone postscript file. Either way, the text can reside as a file on a computer diskette; alternatively, it can reside on a minicomputer or mainframe computer as a file with a URL address and directory path. Many homepages not only contain textual files, but also serve as the front-end service for the information systems (see Figure 4.1).

So far, most attempts to organize the Internet resources and provide access for the users have been done haphazardly. It is not difficult to find electronic indexes to the Internet or other library resources created by individuals with computer skills, creativity, and time to spare on independent projects. Many of such indexing systems are still at the developmental stage.

Monroe (1995) at North Carolina State University categorizes catalogs on or of Internet into the following groups:

- *Catalogs of Internet Resources*—created to organize only Internet resources, often with direct links to the sites of the electronic resources. Examples of this group include the Alex Catalog of Electronic Texts on the Internet[1] and NEEDS courseware database of scientific and engineering courseware on the Internet.

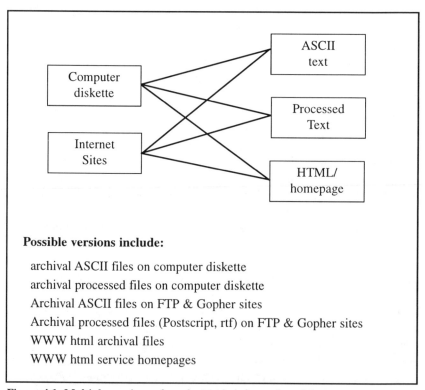

Possible versions include:

archival ASCII files on computer diskette

archival processed files on computer diskette

Archival ASCII files on FTP & Gopher sites

Archival processed files (Postscript, rtf) on FTP & Gopher sites

WWW html archival files

WWW html service homepages

Figure 4.1: Multiple versions of an electronic information object

• *Catalogs with a vendor built-in Web interface but containing no Internet resources*—these are mostly at the demonstration stage. Examples include SIRSI's WebCat,[2] DRA Library Web Information System,[3] and VTLS's HTML Searching Interface.[4]

• *Catalogs with Web to Z39.50 gateway*—this includes library catalogs, such as that of the Library of Congress and Michigan State University's Zweb, that are equipped with Z39.50 client servers, allowing more user-friendly remote retrieval.

• *Catalogs with Web interfaces for traditional materials*—includes that of Carnegie Mellon University and NASA Lunar & Planetary Institute. They provide only surrogate information to traditional nonelectronic collections.

• *Catalogs with gopher gateways*—includes Alex Catalog of Electronic Texts on the Internet (gopher version), Norwegian National Union Catalog, and Eisenhower National Clearinghouse for Math and Science Education.

Internet Indexing Projects

Among all experiments, prototypes, and working projects are a few worth noting here. These are Yahoo at Stanford, Lycos at CMU, Nordic WAIS/World Wide Web Project, EELS (Engineering Electronic Library) at The Swedish University of Technology Libraries, and OCLC's NetFirst.

The first system, Yahoo, originates from Stanford University. It is a system that indexes URL sites for access. It uses humans to do the indexing and therefore maintains some level of quality control over selection of URL sites to be included. The system indexes up to 100 URL addresses per person per day. The index, however, does not attempt to provide detailed information about the content of electronic files themselves.

Lycos of Carnegie Mellon University uses the machine to automatically collect URL addresses for ftp, gopher, and news group sites. With the possibility of indexing any digitized document, it provides potential for quick access to the entire electronic world. It does nothing, however, to help users determine the quality of the contents of the URL sites.

The Nordic WAIS/World Wide Web Project is sponsored by NORDINFO and carried out by The National Technological Library of Denmark and Lund University Library. The objective is to explore the possibilities of improving navigation and searching in the Net. The results, according to its report, include integration of a library system into WWW; automatic detection and classification of WAIS databases, featuring a WWW front-end; automatic detection and

---

930 Engineering Physics (=first level above)

   931 Applied Physics Generally (=actual level)

      931.1 Mechanics (=first level below)

         931.2 Physical Properties of Gases, Liquids and Solids

---

Figure 4.2: Partial screen of the ELLS browsing feature

indexing of Nordic WWW pages; and support for multi-database searching and relevance feedbacks.[5]

The EELS (Engineering Electronic Library) project, currently under development, is sponsored by The Swedish University of Technology Libraries.[6] The best covered subject areas so far are physics, mathematics, energy, computer engineering, general engineering and cold region research. One unique feature of this system is its classified approach to browsing EELS. The system provides the user with a hierarchical subject classificatory structure as a menu of choice, using the Engineering Information Inc. EI classification (Figure 4.2).

A new service recently announced this year through OCLC is NetFirst. According to its news release, NetFirst automatically collects and verifies the Internet resources it gathers, and utilizes conventional abstracting and indexing practices done by humans (Jul 1995b). It contains a database of Internet resources including World Wide Web pages, interest groups, library catalogs, ftp sites, Internet services, gopher servers, electronic journals, and newsletters. Each record for an Internet resource contains the bibliographic citation, summary descriptions, and subject headings. Location information is included in the bibliographic records and can be used to connect users to resources of interest.

All of the projects just described are indexing systems with the purpose of indexing the largest amount of electronic resources and providing users quick access and information delivery. None of them involves any strong intent to practice library cataloging as it is currently understood. In all the projects, the emphasis is on fast indexing and speedy access. The issues most important to catalogers, namely quality and completeness of record description, are only peripheral, if addressed at all.

Electronic resources have been cataloged in libraries for more than a decade, using AACR2 Chapter 9, but catalogers dealt with mostly static archival computer files. In 1992, the library cataloging community began its attempt to catalog electronic resources on the Internet. The following three projects depart

46

significantly from existing practice in that they expand the scope of traditional cataloging to include not only archival computer files but also dynamic electronic resources currently in use or under development. These three projects are OCLC Internet Cataloging Resources Project, University of Virginia Library Project, and OCLC Cataloging Internet Project.

In their report, Dillon et al. (1993) state that the objective of the OCLC Internet Cataloging Experiment is to study the nature of electronic information via remote access and its related problems. The project involved creation of MARC records for various types of Internet resources including source/system codes and text files. The records are then made available through remote access via ftp sites. The project results in a proposal for a new MARC Field 856, which was later approved by MARBI, and a drafting of new cataloging guidelines for organizing Internet resources.

In 1992, the University of Virginia Library established an Electronic Text Center, which is charged with the tasks of digitizing its literature collection, including Old English texts, the Chadwyck-Healy English poetry database, the *Patrologia Latina* database, the *Oxford English Dictionary*, 2nd ed., and the complete works of Shakespeare and of Thomas Jefferson. The digital text is processed through SGML, TEI, Web-interface, HTML. At the time when the document is marked up for electronic storage, a TEI header is also created to record bibliographic data. Meanwhile, a MARC record is created under this project for each electronic document using AACR2, LCRI, OCLC documentation. The result of the project is a database of bibliographic records in MARC format for its digital library (Gaynor 1994).

At the time when OCLC finished its Internet Cataloging Experiment in 1993, a follow-up project, called OCLC Cataloging Internet Project, was initiated. Among the project's goals are identification, selection, and cataloging of Internet resources (Jul 1995c). The resulting records comply with MARC and AACR2 standards, and are suitable for loading into national, regional, or local library catalogs. As of today, the project has more than 170 participant libraries that each produces an average of two or three records per week.

As one examines the MARC records, it is clear that the main types of the electronic resources cataloged under this project are Internet systems and services, and single bibliographic entities with URL addresses. A commonly recognized policy is to catalog those Internet resources that are locally owned, such as the homepages of the local library catalog, or those that are of local interest. Reference tools considered useful to local users are next on the priority list, followed by professional tools available on the Internet. Participating libraries are also encouraged to create multiple 856 fields for multiple versions of an electronic document (Sha 1995). Cataloging under the OCLC Internet Cataloging Project is done in accordance with AACR2, Chapter 9 and their related LCRIs, MARC formats, OCLC's *Cataloging Internet Resources: A Manual and Practical Guide* (Olson 1995), and *Guidelines for the Use of Field 856*, published by the Library of Congress (1995).

Issues Affecting the Organization of the Internet World

Compared to the various indexing projects described earlier, the three fore-going projects deal with only a very small amount of Internet resources. Each of the three projects produces a separate bibliographic database of MARC records often without actual links to the electronic resources themselves. This situation highlights some of the issues in current attempts to organize the electronic world.

The first issue is the separation of a bibliographic record and its primary electronic source. Electronic files can be created by almost anyone who has a word processor or a scanner, an Internet address, or a homepage. At any time, the organizers (indexers or catalogers) feel like they are chasing a runaway train, catching a little bit at a time and watching the train get longer and go faster. Under almost all current projects, the record created is separated from the electronic text itself, making it essential to establish a link between the primary text and the surrogate for each case.

The second issue involves the time and labor intensive MARC cataloging records. Creating a MARC record is a time consuming and labor intensive process. There is no assurance that the cost of creating a record is worth the doing when the contents of the electronic resources are in many cases unstable or even questionable.

The third issue is the uncontrolled quality of Internet indexes available. Most Internet indexes were created for the purpose of capturing the most addresses and providing the most links to electronic data. There is no consistency in indexing, nor is there a minimum standard for record description in all cases.

MARC

      008 ... eng

      0411 laenglhspa

      546 laTranslated from Spanish.

SGML like coding

      [lang]eng[trans]spa

Figure 4.3: A Comparison of MARC vs. SGML coding (Branch 1995)

48

The fourth issue relates to the often duplicate effort in creating MARC records and SGML codes. Some systems (such as the University of Virginia project) have tried to create both the SGML/TEI header and the MARC record for each electronic document; both contain bibliographic data. This represents duplication of coding and twice as much processing effort. An example is the treatment of language text; provisions in both SGML coding and MARC tags allow for language treatment, as seen in Figure 4.3. Either one is sufficient for the record. To have both appears redundant.

The volatility of electronic resources is another issue. Because of the ease and speed of production of electronic resources, the index links created for accessing the resources often are just as volatile. No matter how fast the system can index Internet resources, electronic resources appear and disappear even faster. Operating systems are upgraded; files are moved to new sites and assigned new addresses; and the link between any electronic file and its bibliographic record may become invalid at anytime without notice. To solve this problem, some suggest a passive approach—let the users find out for themselves and report the invalid links found. Others would demand that the electronic publishers notify libraries when changes of URL addresses occur. A third approach, suggested by Dodge, Marx, and Pfeiffenberger (1995), uses a computer program to conduct automatic checking regularly to ensure that the links remain valid.

What Should Cataloging Be in the Electronic World?

Given the issues, it is obvious that cataloging in the electronic world can no longer be done in the traditional way. The question is: What do we want to see in the future of cataloging? or, What is the acceptable norm of organization for the electronic world if not cataloging as usual?

To answer, one can begin by looking at the kinds of electronic entities involved in the process of organization. There are at least six: local documents, remote documents, bibliographic data of any document, the citations or references used in a document, locally created bibliographic records, and remotely accessible surrogate files.

When considering local or remotely accessible electronic documents, it is important to consider the document as full text with any possible illustrations and/or graphic elements. It is more likely the documents will contain labels of some markup language, such as HTML. For the bibliographic data of a document, it is important to consider both the information already existing in the document as well as what could be added during the cataloging process. It is also important to consider both the bibliographic records of the document and the bibliographic elements provided in the citations of a document that could be used as indexing pointers to other related documents. The local surrogate files must be considered together with the remotely accessible surrogate files. Without simultaneous access to both local and remote surrogate files, the system loses one of its most valuable functions as an electronic surrogate system.

In addition to the essential entities of electronic resources, one must also consider the following factors in the future of organizing electronic resources. First is the dynamic nature of producing electronic files. In the Web environment, a file is normally created on a local computer using a word processor. The file, once completed, is marked up using an HTML markup editor. Graphics and TEI headers are often inserted during the markup process. The file is then uploaded to a homepage and given a URL address. Although many files with HTML remain as text-based files, many others contain additional hypertext nodes in the text and the citations that serve as pointers to local and remote URL addresses of other related files.

One of the features of current electronic indexes that must be retained in a successful future cataloging system is the need for fast indexing and speedy access. With the rate at which electronic files and homepages are created on the Internet, the current productivity level in creating MARC records for electronic resources is simply unacceptably low.

Yet one must address the issue of maintaining a certain level of quality among the records and the indexing structures. Standards should be enforced to ensure providing a minimum level of bibliographic data in each description. Sophisticated search keys through controlled vocabularies, classification systems, and name authority control must be made available to the users through an intelligent interface.

A Cataloging Model for the Electronic World

Based on all the factors considered, the following model is proposed as the direction of cataloging in the future of the electronic world. As an electronic document is prepared for adding to, say, an Internet URL site, it is marked in electronic markup languages, such as HTML. In place of the TEI header commonly used in today's markup process, an expanded markup header can be created with human intervention as a cataloging record of the document. The human markup editor, armed with cataloging knowledge and familiarity with markup language syntax, can provide necessary information for the bibliographic description. The electronic system automatically verifies authoritative forms of access points using its intelligent knowledge base. Meanwhile, hypertext nodes are created for the electronic text by marking keywords within the text as well as its citations. At this point, the process of the electronic information object is complete.

The next step is to store the electronic file on a URL site with other local files. During this process, the system extracts the catalog record from the file's header, which is automatically added to the system's local catalog. The system's local catalog is linked with other local and remote surrogate files through homepages, which allows users to get instant access to both. With the connection completed, the catalog essentially becomes an invisible network with links between local library resources and remote databases, and allows users to access information without regard to its physical or time constraints.

Whenever the file needs revision, the markup language editor not only updates the content of the file but also the expanded cataloging header. When the document is moved, its URL address is changed, either by the system automatically or by the human markup editor. When the file is deleted, the expanded cataloging header disappears from the system with the file, thus closing the link between the file and the rest of the electronic world with a message that the file is no longer available.

Characteristics of Cataloging in the Electronic World

Several unique features characterize this proposed cataloging model for the electronic world. Cataloging records exist with(in) the electronic source files, and are not separated from them. The surrogate file in essence is a collection of records with real-time links to the source files themselves. For the system to generate a correct TEI header for the MARC record, the system must also possess the capability of automatic verification and automatic authority control.

One of the important components of cataloging in this model is the integration of associative indexing found in a hypertext environment. At the time the document is marked up for storage and presentation in the electronic format, the text as well as its citations are also marked up with hypertext nodes to be used as indexing pointers. In this model of the future, cataloging and indexing are not two separate steps, but one integral process done at the time of markup editing. The markup language editor is the cataloger and the indexer. The three become one. This process of markup/cataloging/indexing can be a decentralized process, done by individuals within or without an institution, such as a cataloging department.

What Does It Take to Get There?

Catalogers have been using electronic resources as the prime avenue for updating their professional knowledge. Many cataloging tools are regularly updated and posted on a URL site for free access, and more will be seen in the future. Catalogers have also utilized electronic resources as a tool for shared cataloging. Both the electronic update of cataloging knowledge and cooperative cataloging via the Web are not new. Catalogers will continue taking full advantage of these features.

The key to realizing this proposed model of future organization of electronic resources is to integrate the task of cataloging, indexing, and markup editing. To keep up with the growing pace of electronic resources requires greater flexibility in traditional cataloging quality and standards so as to improve productivity. Flexibility may appear to compromise current cataloging quality, but the payoff will be more records and speedier access. Associative indexing will become an integral part of cataloging knowledge.

Catalogers will have to be comfortable not only with using subject headings lists or classification systems, but also with alternative indexing structures, such as hypertext indexing and electronic markup languages. The ability to use markup languages, such as SGML or HTML, is essential for catalogers to participate in the production process of electronic resources. Internet searching will become an integral part of library research. It is as important as learning to search OCLC or one's own online catalog.

Cataloging can no longer be a rigid process separated from other methods of organization. In an electronic world, it should be an integral part of authorship/editorship. In practice, cataloging and markup editing should be merged into one process. Catalogers will be involved in the production and maintenance of electronic resources on the Internet. People who are currently involved in authoring and editing Internet resources will be involved in the process of organization. This proposed model of organization in the electronic world represents an integrated approach to production and organization of electronic resources: it moves catalogers from the sideline of the electronic world to center stage.

Endnotes

1. Homepage available at URL: http://www.lib.ncsu.edu/stacks/alex-index.html
2. Homepage available at URL: http://www.sirsi.com/webcattoc.html
3. Homepage available at URL: http://www.dra.com/dralibrary.html
4. Homepage available at URL: http://www.vtls.com/dev/VTLS_Search.html
5. Homepage available at URL: http://www.ub2.lu.se/W4.html
6. Homepage available at URL: http://www.ub2.lu.se/eel/eelhome.html

References

Branch, F. L. 1995. Re: MARC Record Structure. [E-mail to INTERCAT listserv, online.] February 28. Available on INTERCAT archives at listserv@oclc.org.

Cutter, C. A. 1904. *Rules for a Dictionary Catalog.* 4th ed. Washington: Government Printing Office.

Dillon, M. et al. 1993. *Accessing Information on the Internet: Toward Providing Library Services for Computer-Mediated Communication.* Dublin, OH: OCLC Online Computer Library Center.

Dodge, C., B. Marx, and H. Pfeiffenberger. 1995. Web cataloguing through cache exploitation and steps toward consistency maintenance. *Computer Networks and ISDN Systems.* 27(6): 1003-1008.

Drabenstott, K. M. 1994. *Analytical Review of the Library of the Future.* Washington: Council on Library Resources.

Gaynor, E. 1994. Cataloging electronic texts: the University of Virginia Library experience. *LRTS* 38(4): 403-413.

Gorman, M. and P. Winkler. 1988. *Anglo-American Cataloguing Rules,* 2d ed. rev. Chicago: American Library Association.

Jul, E. 1995a. Integrated Access. [E-mail to INTERCAT listserv, online.] March 24. Available on INTERCAT archives at listserv@oclc.org.

———. 1995b. NetFirst. [E-mail to INTERCAT listserv, online.] April 7. Available on INTERCAT archives at listserv@oclc.org.

———. 1995c. Getting a Sense of Involvement. [E-mail to INTERCAT listserv, online.] April 13. Available on INTERCAT archives at listserv@oclc. org.

Library of Congress. 1995. *Guidelines for the Use of Field 856.* Washington: Library of Congress.

Monroe, H. 1995. Library Catalogs of Internet Resources. [E-mail to INTERCAT listserv, online.] April 18. Available of INTERCAT archives at listserv@oclc.org. Also available at URL: http://www.lib.ncsu.edu/staff/morgan/alcuin/wwwed-catalogs.html

Olson, N. B. 1995. *Cataloging Internet Resources: A Manual and Practical Guide.* Dublin, OH: OCLC Online Computer Library Center. Also available on Anonymous FTP: ftp.rsch.oclc.org/pub/internet_cataloging_project/Manual.txt.

Sha, V. 1995. Guidelines for Cataloging Electronic Resources. [E-mail to INTERCAT listserv, online.] March 28. Available on INTERCAT archives at listserv@oclc.org.

Stewart, B. 1995. Summary of replies to WWW access for technical services. [E-mail to LITA-L listserv, online.] March 27. Available on LITA-L archives at listserv@uicvm.bitnet.

Chapter 5

Chinese Electronic Publishing on the Internet: Technical Approaches

Huijie Chen
Pennsylvania State University Harrisburg

Hong Xu
University of Illinois at Urbana Champaign

Abstract

On the Internet, electronic signals are transmitted in ones and zeros regardless of whether the content is in Chinese, English, or any other language. The binary codes of the computer network should ideally make electronic publishing in Chinese as straightforward as that in English. The fundamental differences between Chinese and English computing, however, make implementation of electronic publishing in Chinese more complicated. This chapter discusses issues and solutions related to text encoding/decoding for Chinese-language electronic publishing on the Internet. A case study of the first Chinese-language electronic journal on the Internet illustrates these issues and solutions.

Electronic Publishing on the Internet

Two elements are essential for electronic publishing on the Internet: electronic signals as the distribution media for text, and computer networks as the transmission channel for text. The diagram of Figure 5.1 shows a model for electronic publishing on computer networks.

Implementation of an encoding/decoding process always takes place behind the scenes as part of electronic publishing on computer networks. First, text prepared by the author is encoded into electronic signals by a character code table or by image attributes, then it is distributed through computer networks. ASCII (American Standard Code for Information Interchange) is the code table

55

primarily designed for English-language text. For example, the letter "A" may be encoded into the ASCII code number 065 or a dot matrix pattern. Either the number 065 or the dot matrix must be converted into zeros and ones before transmission (Table 5.1). At the reader's end, electronic signals are decoded back to text before presentation for viewing.

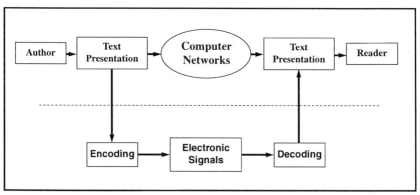

Table 5.1. Model for Electronic Publishing

Since the debut of the Internet, several different communication methods have been employed for electronic publishing, including e-mail distribution lists, newsgroups, FTP, Gopher, and the World Wide Web (WWW). Our discussion centers upon the way text is distributed and viewed in each of these different methods. For English text, these methods are summarized in Table 5.2.

Certainly each of these methods may be used for electronic publishing of Chinese text. Due to the nature of Chinese computing, however, Chinese text requires additional encoding and decoding before it can be distributed and viewed on the Internet, which is an English-dominated computing environment.

DISTRIBUTION METHOD	TRANSMISSION MODE	VIEWING MODE
E-mail distribution list	Text	Online
Newsgroup	Text	Online
FTP	Text/Graphic	Offline
Gopher	Text/Graphic	Online/Offline
WWW	Text/Graphic	Online/Offline

Table 5.2. Summary of English Text Transmission Methods

Thus, the online attributes listed in Table 5.2 for English text may not be applicable for Chinese text.

Chinese Text Encoding: Character Based vs. Graphic Based

Chinese characters are composed of sets of pictographic or ideographic symbols. The language has several thousand characters that are essential for general communication purposes. For electronic publishing on computer networks, the key issue for authors using Chinese, who also play the role of information distributor, is whether to transmit Chinese text by character codes or by image codes. Transmitting Chinese text by character codes uses the characters' positional attributes in a defined character set, a code table. Transmitting by image codes uses the characters' graphic attributes as they appear in print.

Encoding each character by graphic image requires a large number of data bits. For example, a 16 by 16 bitmap matrix, a very low resolution for most Chinese characters, requires 256 (16x16) bits, which is equivalent to 32 bytes, for a single character. In comparison, Chinese characters can be coded in 16-bit (2-byte) patterns with a defined character set (Table 5.1). Each character takes only a two-byte space. Obviously, transmitting Chinese by image attributes requires more bandwidth. The author must convert the text into a graphic format before distribution, and the reader requires a general purpose graphic viewer at the receiving end.

On the other hand, transmitting Chinese text by character codes requires a standard character set. A standard character set consists of individual characters and their defined sequential arrangement. A character set is systematically arranged and then coded for computing, one positional code for each character. In theory, using 16-bit patterns accommodates up to 65,536 (2^{16}) code spaces. (The reason for using 16-bit combinations, rather than any number between 9 and 15, is to ensure compatibility with the word length in the English computing environment.)

A standard character set is accompanied by a font file, which renders images for all characters in the set. In the font file, each character appears only once, but all characters are included. Understandably, the size of the font file is considerably larger even at a moderate resolution. All Chinese text files, when generated by a computer, are normally stored in character codes. When displaying a text file, a Chinese viewer is needed to render the text presentation by linking character codes to the font file.

A major problem is that several Chinese character sets exist, including the GB, BIG5, and Unicode sets. The size, content, and arrangement of these character sets differ. A Chinese text file encoded by one character set standard becomes completely illegible when viewed under the coding environment for another character set. Thus, transmitting Chinese text in character codes requires that both the author and the reader have access to the same character set, or have the capability of converting between different character sets.

Another difficulty arises related to using 16-bit character codes for Chinese text on the Internet. For Chinese computing, 16-bit coding means full use of every bit in an 8-bit byte. In order to be compatible with the English environment, Chinese characters are normally coded with ASCII codes ranging from 128 to 255, whose highest bit is 1. Unfortunately, the 8-bit data pattern is not fully supported by computer networks, especially under text distribution mode. While the Internet is capable of transmitting full 8-bit bytes, there are several bottlenecks, including mainframes, terminals, and terminal emulation applications that only support 7-bit data transmission or that set default to 7-bit data transmission. All 8-bit data passing through this environment, such as e-mail messages, are automatically shifted to 7-bit data, which strips off the highest bit in each byte. When this happens, it is impossible to restore a text that contains both 7-bit and 8-bit bytes. Thus, Chinese electronic publishing should also ensure the integrity of all 8-bit data over the network.

Chinese electronic publishing on the Internet also faces a trade-off between content and format. Character-based coding ensures that the textual content can be used for further manipulation, such as searching and editing. However, due to the lack of a standard for Chinese text formatting for font sizes and styles, the only way to display Chinese text with special effects generated by the author is to code it in graphic mode.

The final concern at the reader's end is whether to view Chinese text in online mode or offline mode. Obviously, online is more convenient for the reader who has access to better machine resources, such as an online Chinese viewer, online graphic viewer, or a Chinese environment. On the other hand, offline still requires that the reader have a general purpose Chinese viewer or a graphic viewer, which normally is more accessible.

Various Approaches for Chinese Text Encoding

One of the unique issues for Chinese electronic publishing on the Internet is text encoding/decoding. The way the text is coded determines the way it will be distributed and viewed. Chinese text encoding methods can be grouped into four types, as described below.

Native Coding

This approach uses the native codes of the standard character sets, such as GB or BIG5, to distribute Chinese text. Text can only be distributed when an application, such as FTP and WWW, can directly handle full 8-bit data.

Generally, only plain text is transmitted. For online use, Chinese environment support, such as a Chinese DOS or Windows, is necessary. The World Wide Web is the best distribution channel for Chinese text in native code. For offline use, FTP is the most suitable approach for distribution. A Chinese viewer or Chinese environment support is also needed for offline viewing.

Shifted Coding

As a variety of native coding, shifted coding bypasses the high-bit shifting problem on computer networks when delivering the text in character codes. Several shifting methods have been implemented so far. Commonly used methods include UU encoding, HZ encoding, and ZW encoding.

UU Encoding. The UU encoding method is commonly used for sending any binary file in text mode. This approach separates each two 8-byte data elements into three 6-bit segments. Then, each 6-bit segment is stuffed into one byte with the highest bit always a 0. In many platforms, any UUENCODE programs can be used for this purpose. The encoded file needs to be decoded with UUDECODE programs before it can be viewed with a general purpose Chinese viewer. This approach can be used for any type of Chinese coding system, such as GB and BIG5. Generally, it adds about one third more overhead data to the original text; and it works for e-mail lists and newsgroup distribution. Limited by the encoding and decoding process, this approach is suitable for offline use.

ZW Encoding. Designed for GB-coded Chinese text only, this approach precedes each text line with a text string of "zW" as an identifier tag, then checks the highest bit in each byte. If the high-bit is 1, it shifts the bit to 0. If the high-bit is 0, it attaches a space character (ASCII 032) after the byte. The overhead amount depends on the original text. If the original text is all Chinese, a maximum of 3 to 5 percent of overhead data is added. When the file contains mostly English text, close to 100 percent of overhead data is added. There is a TSR utility running under the DOS environment for viewing ZW-encoded GB text online. This approach is suitable for online use of e-mail, newsgroups, and text-based Gopher and WWW.

HZ Encoding. Also designed for GB-coded Chinese text, HZ encoding marks up a string of 8-bit bytes (ASCII code 128-255) with a pair of text strings ("~{" and "~}") as identifier tags, then it shifts each high bit from one to zero. For strings of 7-bit bytes (ASCII code below 128), no tags are added. The amount of overhead data depends on the original text. In theory, if the original text is all Chinese, only one pair of identification tags is needed. If the original text is all English, no tag is needed. With this flexibility, the overhead data is minimized in every situation. There is also a TSR utility running under the DOS environment for viewing HZ-encoded GB text online. Like ZW encoding, this approach is suitable for online use of e-mail, newsgroups, and text-based Gopher and WWW.

Encapsuled Encoding

Using the PostScript format, this approach transmits a formatted graphic file in text mode. After formatting Chinese text, the author generates a PostScript file by using a PostScript printer driver or a special converting utility. The resultant file can be distributed via e-mail, newsgroups, and text-based Gopher and WWW. The reader needs to have access to a PostScript printer or a PostScript viewer in order to render the graphic image. This approach does not require a Chinese viewer or Chinese environment support, and it can preserve the special effects generated by the author. Although it is possible to send via e-mail, a PostScript file is distributed more efficiently by FTP due to the tremendous amount of the overhead data. Therefore, this approach is mainly for offline use.

Graphic Encoding

This approach treats Chinese text in a purely graphic way. After formatting the text, the author generates a graphic file in a format such as BMP, GIF, JPG, or PCX. The resultant file can be distributed via FTP or WWW, and used either online or offline. As discussed above, it requires more bandwidth, but it can preserve the author's special effects. Recent progress in image compression also makes it possible to distribute relatively large images. The only requirement is a general purpose graphic viewer at the reader's end. For example, any graphic Web browser can be used for viewing an image-coded Chinese text on the Internet.

Table 5.3 summarizes all the encoding methods discussed above.

A Case Study: HXWZ

Hua Xia Wen Zai (HXWZ), known in English as *CND-Chinese Magazine*, is one of the electronic journals published by CND International, Inc. Founded in 1989 by a group of Chinese student volunteers in the U.S. and Canada, CND owns the world's largest e-mail distribution list. According to CND's statistics, the number of direct subscribers in May 1995 exceeded 35,000, representing fifty countries and regions in Africa, Asia, Oceania, Europe, North America, and South America. CND provides five sections of English news services and one Chinese publication. All CND publications are distributed without charge via e-mail lists, newsgroups, FTP, Gopher, and WWW.

CND began publication of *HXWZ* in April 1991 as the first electronic journal on the Internet in Chinese text. The two main goals of *HXWZ* are (1) to facilitate the free circulation of news and information in order to promote Chinese culture and to serve overseas Chinese students and scholars; and (2)

TYPE	FORMAT	APPROACH	OVERHEAD	MODE	REQUIREMENT
Native encoding	GB, BIG5	FTP	none	offline	general purpose Chinese viewer
		Gopher, WWW	none	online	Chinese environment
Shifted encoding	uuencoded (UU)	E-mail, newsgroup	medium	offline	UU decoding utility and general purpose Chinese viewer
	HZ, ZW	E-mail, newsgroup, text based Gopher & WWW	minimum	online	HZ/ZW online decoding utility
Graphic encoding	GIF, BMP, PCX, JPG, etc	WWW	medium–maximum	online	General purpose graphic WWW viewer
Encapsuled encoding	PostScript (PS)	E-mail, newsgroup, FTP	maximum	offline	PostScript viewer/printer

Table 5.3. Summary of Chinese Text Encoding/Decoding Approaches

to become a medium to improve and popularize modern information transmission technology in China and to promote computerization of Chinese information processing. *HXWZ* carries China-related news items and other selected essays on Chinese politics, economics, culture, education, and literature. With an average length of 45,000 to 50,000 bytes of native text codes for each issue, *HXWZ* is published on a weekly basis, with irregular supplements about once a month.

As a pioneer in Chinese electronic publishing, CND has successfully applied many coding methods for distributing *HXWZ* to meet different needs. From the beginning, *HXWZ* was delivered with UU encoding to its direct subscribers. In this case, readers need to extract each e-mail message containing the UU-encoded file, download the file to a personal computer, convert it to a GB file with a UU-decode program, then view it with a general purpose Chinese viewer.

HXWZ's readership on the direct distribution list grew from 2,200 in June 1991, to more than 15,800 in May 1995. Table 5.4 lists the *HXWZ* subscribers by text coding format during selected months. Statistics before 1995 are recorded in CND's readership report of September 13, 1994. Figures for 1995 were reported in March 6, 1995, issue of *CND-Global* (URL:ftp://cnd.cnd.org/pub/cnd-global/1995.1-6/cnd-global.95-03-05.Z).

Coding Method	1991 (June)	1992 (March)	1993 (March)	1994 (March)	1995 (March)
GB	2,201	4,293	9,900	11,793	15,800
HZ			639	3,034	

Table 5.4. Number of HXWZ Subscribers per Mailing Lists

During the period from 1992 to 1994, another *HXWZ* distribution list came to service by delivering *HXWZ* in HZ-encoded format. This distribution list actually started with two subscribers in December 1992. Since one can directly read *HXWZ* with an online HZ viewer, this list quickly attracted thousands of readers. In July 1994, the number of subscribers reached 9,000. The list was interrupted in July 1994 due to the loss of access to the listserv host machine. Since then, CND has made the HZ-encoded *HXWZ* accessible at CND's FTP and WWW servers.

Anonymous FTP for GB, BIG5, and PostScript files is the way CND provides current and back issues of *HXWZ*. To take advantage of PostScript format, *HXWZ* volunteers take additional steps to format the magazine for better presentation, adding photo pictures and other graphic materials, for example.

CND's 1995 records showed that each week, there were 8,900 FTP requests for the GB version and 4,600 requests for the PostScript version.

Financed by readers' donations, CND set up a Gopher server (URL:gopher://gopher.cnd.org) in 1993 and a WWW server (URL:http://www.cnd.org) in 1994 for all CND publications, including *HXWZ*. Both servers have English interfaces, HZ-encoded Chinese interfaces, and graphic interfaces. Current and back issues of *HXWZ* are available in all GB, BIG5, HZ, and PostScript formats. In May 1994, *HXWZ* became available on the Web in GIF format, which is supported by all graphic Web browsers. Thus, for the first time, *HXWZ* readers can read the magazine without using any Chinese viewing systems. Each week, there are about 6,000 visits for the GIF version.

Table 5.5 summarizes the average number of weekly accesses to CND FTP and WWW servers for *HXWZ* in different coding formats, based on the data reported in the CND-Global anniversary issues and the CND Web statistical reports.

Coding and Access Methods	1991	1992	1993	1994	1995
GB (FTP)	500	1,000	4,500	6,700	8,900
PS (FTP)	300	1,000	3,000	3,000	,600
HZ (WWW)				30	1,066
GIF (WWW)				5,000	6,000
GB (WWW)					245

Table 5.5. Average Number of Accesses to HXWZ via FTP/WWW per Week

Conclusion

Like the end-user base for the whole Internet, the readership for Chinese electronic publishing on the Internet is growing constantly. With such a broad potential readership, none of the encoding/decoding methods alone can satisfy all readers' needs. Although people tend to follow the path of least resistance to get the information they need, different readers also value various characteristics, such as online viewing or saving bandwidth, over others in order to meet different information needs in different circumstances.

Electronic publishing in Chinese has some unique difficulties, especially in the area of text encoding/decoding. We believe that the key to success is to ensure that text is coded in the various ways readers can handle. Those who want to work on electronic publishing for Chinese text on the Internet need to be prepared for additional challenges. CND's experience shows that when multiple encoding methods are adapted simultaneously to meet different user needs, readership increases greatly.

Note: The authors are grateful to CND volunteers, especially Mr. Wei Lin and Mr. Bo Xiong, for providing the CND statistics.

References

Lunde, Ken. 1993. *Understanding Japanese Information Processing*. Sebastopol, CA: O'Reilly & Associates.

The Unicode Consortium. 1992. *The Unicode Standards: Worldwide Character Encoding, Version 1.0, Volume 2*. Reading, MA: Addison-Wesley.

SECTION TWO

ELECTRONIC PUBLISHING APPLICATIONS

Chapter 6

Electronic News

Michael A. Shepherd
Dalhousie University

C.R. Watters
Acadia University

F.J. Burkowski
University of Waterloo

Abstract

Electronic news delivery systems exploit communication and multimedia technologies to integrate newspapers, television news clips, and radio news clips into personalized editions for subscribers. This chapter differentiates electronic news from newspaper databases and presents a three-layer architecture for the news sources, news management, and news reader functions within the context of digital libraries for electronic news. We describe an ongoing project, a prototype of which was demonstrated successfully at the G7 Economic Summit held in Halifax, Canada, June 14-18, 1995.

Introduction

Research on the use of electronic news as a digital library is a major component of an ongoing research program for the development of an electronic news delivery system that exploits the promised high bandwidth, switched, interactive communication facilities of the "information highway." [4, 5, 12, 13] Initially based on a newspaper metaphor (Figure 6.1), the system exploits communication and multimedia technologies to integrate other news sources, such as newscasts and video clips, with the text backbone. The newspaper text and photographs are from The Halifax Herald Limited and the television news videos are from Atlantic Television System. The system will provide selective content delivery based on individual and group profiles, hypertext links into

Figure 6.1: Front Page

archival and external data, continuous coverage of live news events, interactive objects, and consumer-oriented "smart" advertising.

Such an electronic news application is well suited to the promised broadband networks in that:

- the wide distribution of such a communications network is consistent with the mass distribution of news;
- the switched nature of such a network will allow for the customization or personalization of the news format and content;
- the high communications bandwidth is consistent with the multimodal nature of news (text, photographs, video clips, live broadcast, etc.);
- the two-way nature of the network opens avenues for interactive and targeted advertising and for interactive items such as bridge hands, crossword puzzles, and classified ads.

Initial prototype clients have been developed using data that include television news video clips and newspaper text and photos. An abstract data representation was developed for the integration of layout, syntactic, and semantic

68

information from a variety of sources for the dynamic presentation and manipulation of the news items.

The remainder of this chapter briefly outlines this electronic news project and introduces an architecture for digital library support of integration of electronic news.

Newspaper Databases

A distinction must be made between newspaper databases and the delivery of electronic news. Generally, newspaper databases with on-line access do not present the news in a recognized news format. These systems are essentially document retrieval systems in which individual news articles are treated as discrete units, i.e., stories are treated as documents. [9, 10] In accessing these newspaper database systems, the user task is to satisfy an articulated information need. Retrieval is accomplished by the user formulating a Boolean query or selecting from menus of headings.

Electronic News

Certain key concepts differentiate electronic news products from newspaper databases. These differences consist of the delivery method, the use of a recognizable news format, and task.

Delivery method. Electronic news will be delivered to the home and/or workplace as are today's newspapers and television and radio news. Broadband networks will deliver the news, even to wireless PIAs. [6]

Format. These systems will deliver the news in a recognizable format, initially a newspaper format with integrated video and sound clips. While there is some concern over the acceptability of the newspaper in electronic versus paper form,[10] the electronic form appears to be inevitable. Although the newspaper metaphor is likely to be only the initial interface as the paradigm continues to evolve,[1] it is a well-recognized and nearly universal platform for news delivery. In addition to this project,[4, 5, 12, 13] the Newspace[3] and is-News[11] projects maintain the newspaper metaphor for electronic news delivery.

Task. Perhaps most important, newspaper databases and electronic news differ in the concept of the readers' task. The task in accessing a newspaper database is to satisfy an articulated information need, whereas the task in accessing electronic news is to satisfy an unarticulated need, often to simply find out what is happening.

Features of an Electronic News System

Our research has focused on the development of a prototype electronic news delivery system, which includes the automatic linking of news items on the same event but from different sources (including different media), the creation of stereotyped editions of integrated news items, client/server architectures, and user interfaces. The system presents news at the user interface in the newspaper metaphor, exploiting broadband communication and multimedia technologies to integrate video, photo, and audio news items with the text backbone. The information content and functionality of such a system, when fully employed, will include core content, stereotyped content based on group profiles, individual profiles, supplemental content, interactive and real-time objects, and access to digital libraries.

Electronic News as a Digital Library

Electronic news is a particularly interesting basis for a distributed digital library. News is information about events, people, and places. It has a sense of immediacy about it; yesterday's news is old news. Yet, yesterday's news is important in defining and understanding today's news. For instance, a single event such as the Olympic Games is reported on before, during, and after the event. So, a digital library of electronic news must support both electronic news and news databases, whether the news databases are archives of print, television, or radio news. Television and radio news are both read from scripts, so this textual information must be included in the digital library, along with the actual broadcast.

Attributes of News Items

Both structural and semantic attributes of news items can be identified and marked up using the Universal Text Format (UTF).[2, 8] An instantiation of the Standard Generalized Markup Language (SGML), the UTF is a proposed news industry standard for the interchange of textual material between news agencies and their clients. A UTF marked-up item can be embedded in an envelope defined by the Information Interchange Model, which can accommodate all types of data, including text, graphics, audio and video. Proponents of the UTF include publishers of newspapers such as *The New York Times*, the *Miami Herald*, and the *Chicago Tribune*, and other organizations such as Dow Jones, and the Mead Data Center.

Structural attributes describe the news object itself, much like a bibliographic entry describes the object of reference. Such attributes include the story byline, headline, subheadings, date and time that the object was created, the source of the object, the news organization, the type of the object (text, graphic, video), keywords describing the content, and reference to previous items.

Semantic attributes are drawn from the information within the text of a news item. For instance, the UTF includes markup definition for date and time, location, and the names of people, events, products, companies, etc. It also includes markup for numbers and their units; both within textual news items and within tables such as stock market information and sports box scores.

The UTF markup structure, which is much richer than indicated here, provides a sophisticated information retrieval environment. In addition to retrieval based on such traditional attributes as keywords, names, places, etc., the markup provides possibilities for temporal retrieval and analysis of events and for some numeric processing. In particular, the temporal attributes appear at both the structural and the semantic levels, allowing the user to follow a timeline in the reporting of a news item as well as temporal reasoning based on attributes at the semantic level.

News Delivery and a Digital Library

Gladney, et al. suggest that, "[the] document storage and access software [for a digital library] can be implemented in two layers above a base of file systems and database managers."[7] The lower layer is a resource manager that, among other functions, provides a query interface to browsers and retrieves items from the database managers. The upper layer is a document manager that resides in the user's workstation. The term "document" is used to represent an information item that may be of various media types, possibly a combination of media types. The document manager provides the information model and transforms, combines, and presents documents to the user. Where necessary, applications can bypass the document manager and go directly to the resource manager.

Because many features of an electronic news delivery system depend on access to a digital library of electronic news, an architecture is proposed that integrates the electronic news delivery with a digital library of electronic news. Digital libraries are accessed as document retrieval systems, i.e., by user query. The electronic news system, as described above, requires that news be delivered as stereotyped editions and that users are able to personalize the edition by retrieval based on user profiles and supplemental queries. This necessitates the integration of the delivery function of electronic news with the query function of a digital library. The architecture proposed to integrate these functions has three layers: the news resource layer, the news management layer, and the news reader layer (Figure 6.2). The resource management layer of Gladney, et al. corresponds to the news resource layer of the proposed architecture.[7]

The functions of the document manager layer of Gladney, et al.[7] are split over the news management and the news reader layers in the proposed archi-

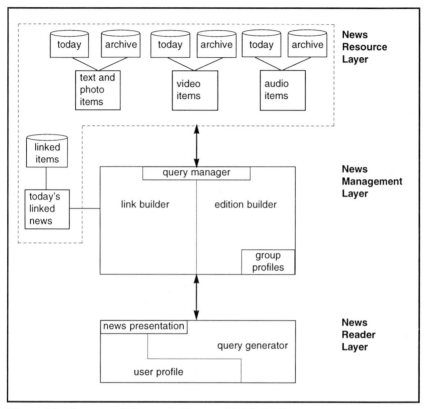

Figure 6.2: Integrated Electronic News and Digital Library

tecture. News items are combined into editions at the news management layer, but the information model and presentation aspects reside in the news reader layer at the user's workstation.

News Resource Layer. This layer comprises multiple news providers of each type of media. All such providers, whether they be print, television or radio media, produce news items for immediate dissemination and then store these items in their own archives. Presumably, some items will be generated and stored in the archives, but never actually distributed. There is usually no cross referencing among news items held in archives by different providers, although there may be cross referencing among items in the same archive or across archives held by the same provider.

Each news resource mounts its archive and the news of the day as a server. The archive and the news of the day can be searched by an information retrieval engine at the server. The use of UTF as a markup language, or even as a switching language, eliminates many problems associated with semantic heterogeneity. Note that today's news, when linked at the news management layer, is also considered as part of the news resource layer.

News Management Layer. In the news management layer of Figure 6.2, vertical lines separating modules indicate that one module does not call the other module for service. Horizontal lines indicate that the higher module calls the lower module for service.

News items of the day are received from the news resource layer. The link builder brings together news items that cover the same topic, regardless of the media type or source. These linked items are stored temporarily and used as a resource. The edition builder generates electronic stereotyped editions of the news, based on the group profiles, from the linked items in the temporary database. These editions are then sent to the appropriate readers at the news reader level.

The query manager responds to requests from the news reader layer for supplemental information. A query may or may not incorporate the individual user profile at the reader layer. The query manager sends this query to the news resource layer. Depending on the type of query, it may request service only from today's linked news items in the temporary database or it may go to all of the news resource managers. The query manager calls the link builder to build links among items retrieved from the news resource layer, if necessary. The query manager then calls the edition builder to generate an edition of the items retrieved in response to the query. In this instance of an individual query, the edition builder does not use the group profiles. These personal query editions are then sent to the requester at the news reader layer.

News Reader Layer. The news reader layer resides in the user's workstation or personal computer. Vertical lines separating modules indicate that one module does not call the other module for service. Horizontal lines indicate that the higher module calls the lower module for service. This layer accepts stereotyped editions of the news and produces personalized editions of the news. This includes dynamic layout of the received news and the requesting of supplemental material based on the user profile or end-user actions.

The news presentation module receives an edition of the news containing core and stereotype news items. In order to personalize the edition, a personal agent based on the user's profile will retrieve items of interest through the query manager in the news management layer. The retrieved items are integrated with the previously received stereotyped edition. In carrying out this function, the news presentation module calls the user profile module and the query generator module.

The user profile module is a dynamically changing outline of the user's interests and the user's preferences for the display style of received news.

The query generator allows the user to request information not contained in the initial stereotyped edition. It may or may not reference the user profile module in generating the query. Results of the query are returned as an edition for presentation by the news presentation module. The user queries may be classified as requests for additional news items related to a particular item in the current edition, either from today's news or from archived news; or as requests for news items on a topic unrelated to any particular news item, either from today's news or from archived news. The query manager retrieves these items from the appropriate news resource servers based on links in the UTF format, or it will submit retrieval requests to the servers in order to satisfy requests for archived news items.

Advertisements

Advertising revenues currently account for approximately 80 percent of a newspaper's revenues and take 40 to 60 percent of its space. Given the size restrictions of a computer screen, more imagination must be used in the design and presentation of ads used in electronic news delivery systems.

To sample this area we have included ads that are buttons, ads that are timed, and ads that are activated whenever a mouse passes over that part of the screen. These include the following:

- Background ads. These are part of the background so that each one is presented briefly each time the user returns to the front page, even when the user has moved another item on top of that ad.
- Icon Ads. Most of the ads used in the prototype are represented by an icon. If the mouse comes within a certain distance of the ad object, the object opens up into a full-sized, full-color ad. Subsequent removal of the mouse or time-out are used to return the ad to its iconic form.
- Animation. The animation of a moving car was used in an earlier prototype. When the user clicked on the ad, the car moved from the distance to a position in the foreground.
- Video. Full-color digitized video ads were used in the G7 prototype.

Figure 6.3 illustrates three different types of ads on one page. The "MT&T Mobility" ad is static. The clock (upper right) blows up to a large full-color ad. The video icon (also upper right) represents a 15-second video ad.

An extremely important feature of such a system is the two-way communications available. System providers will be able to track who views ads, and how often and for how long. Then, they can report the collected information to the advertisers.

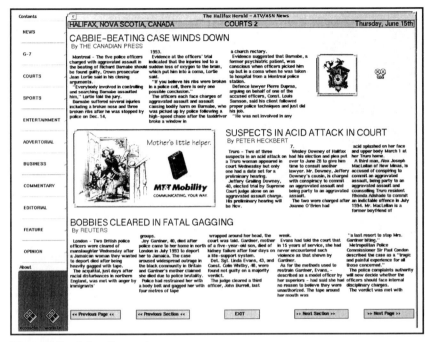

Figure 6.3: Advertisements

Bandwidth Requirements

The delivery of electronic news as proposed above will require a switched, two-way, high-speed communications network. The specifications of such a network will be driven by the size of the video news clips, as opposed to the size of the text files. In order to attain HDTV quality for the videos, it will be necessary to deliver 30 frames per second of 24-bit color video.

Let us assume the following:

- each video frame is 352 x 240 pixels, 24-bit color
- capture and playback at 30 frames per second
- each news video clip lasts 90 seconds
- each news edition has 10 video news clips
- MPEG-2 compression of 30:1
- ATM network of 150 megabits/second.

Based on these assumptions, it will take only approximately twelve seconds to download the videos of a single edition to a single reader. To deliver this news to even 100,000 readers, however, requires 340 hours of total bandwidth.

Increasing the ATM bandwidth to 600 megabits/second and the compression ratio to 90:1 reduces the network transmission time to one second for this single reader. But even those parameters require almost 28 hours of total bandwidth for 100,000 readers.

Let us consider a rather simplistic scenario. Assume that each user has a personal 10-digit network address, the network is a switched tree with 10-way branching, the tree is 10 levels deep, switching is instantaneous, and the time to transmit the above news between switches is one second. In such a scenario, the network could deliver the above news to 10 billion users in only 10 seconds.

More realistically, we need higher bandwidth, higher compression, an efficient network topology, and smart algorithms to determine what items to get and when to get them.

Prototypes

Several prototypes have been developed as part of the research project. The architecture of these systems closely follows the proposed architecture described except for access to digital libraries.

PC-Based Prototype

The first prototype was not networked. The data manipulation was done on a Sun Microsystems workstation in UNIX and the resulting edition downloaded to a personal computer for viewing. The newspaper source data from *The Chronicle-Herald* newspaper was supplied as ASCII text with JPEG photographs. The television news clips were supplied in VHS format by Baton Broadcasting Inc. and digitized during the data manipulation. The reader layer was implemented in Multimedia Toolbook.

G7 Economic Summit

The latest prototype is a fully featured system and was demonstrated at the G7 Economic Summit in Halifax, Canada, June 14-18, 1995. Electronic news was produced and delivered each day. The source data from *The Chronicle-Herald* (published by the Halifax Herald Ltd.)newspaper was supplied as ASCII text with JPEG photographs. The news clips were supplied in VHS format by Atlantic Television System. Both the news management layer and the news reader layer were implemented in a Sun Microsystems UNIX environment.

The news server was located at Dalhousie University and the news items were delivered on demand over a high-speed ATM network to clients located at the conference site. Maritime Telephone & Telegraph provided an OC3 communications line operating at 155 megabits per second, Atlantic Canada Organization for Research Networking provided an ATM switch, and Sun

76

Microsystems of Canada provided a Sparcstation 20. This system permitted the news videos to be delivered on demand at 30 frames per second in 24-bit color.

The newspaper metaphor is presented (Figures 6.1 and 6.3-5) with several stories displaying on each page with room for advertisements, news capsules, and photos. Indices and space overloading techniques were used to maintain the newspaper metaphor functionality in the reduced space of the computer screen.

News indices for the entire edition are generated by the client and can be seen in Figures 6.1 and 6.3-5. The news-item index is generated for each section of the news in standard categories and can be personalized for the particular reader according to sections most frequently read and according to some preferred order. All indices are presented as pull-right menus that show the titles of the stories on each page in that section.

Screen Sharing

A problem with an electronic newspaper format is the restricted space of the computer screen. In order to present multiple items simultaneously, the space allocated to each story on a page is considerably reduced, thereby compounding the annoying fragmentation of longer stories common in printed newspapers. Traditional newspapers make extensive use of continuation to reduce the

Figure 6.4: Exploded Story

amount of page space used by each news item. This permits more items to be introduced on a single page and more ads to appear on a page.

Three different ways of dealing with this problem on the computer are the use of a *More* button to move to another page with additional text, scrollable windows, and exploding windows. An exploding window permits the reader to click on a story and have the entire page overwritten with the full text of the story. A subsequent click returns the page to its original form. The use of a *More* button and the exploding window are more acceptable than scrolling, which can be irritating for large stories. Figure 6.4 is an example of an exploding window. This was obtained by clicking on the text of the story in the lower right corner of the front page (Figure 6.1).

Capsule items common to most newspapers are present in the prototype as headings, which the reader can expand to read the full capsule.

Photos and videos can be shown either always or only upon reader request. Unfortunately both videos and photos take up a considerable amount of screen area. In the PC-based prototype, photos (except on the front page) and videos are available on demand. The photo buttons are thumbprint iconized versions of

Figure 6.5: Television News

the photos themselves. When enlarged for viewing, the layout placement of a photo must not cover the related story.

Integration of Television News

Figure 6.5 shows the video overlay on the screen for television news. Full VCR-type controls on the video window are provided as shown. In addition to the problems of storage, communications, and decompression, the system must devise a method to identify the contents of a video before the user actually chooses to view it. In this prototype, the presence of a video is indicated by a movie projector icon. Different colors indicate different contents: a blue icon indicates that the video is about the same story with which it is physically integrated on the screen; a red icon indicates that the video is not associated with any particular story, but is relevant to the section (e.g., sports) in which it appears; a green icon is an advertisement. This method is not totally satisfactory, but we have not yet addressed the problem.

Summary

Although the delivery of electronic news is well-suited for exploiting the promised high bandwidth, switched, interactive communication facilities of the information highway, the system's effectiveness depends on its capability to both deliver the news and provide access to digital libraries of electronic news data. Our initial investigations and prototyping experiences indicate that many open questions remain, including appropriate client/server architectures, abstract data representations, the use of personal agents, use of the UTF, amounts of information retrieved, categorization of news content, and automatic updating of personal user profiles.

Acknowledgements

We would like to thank the Natural Sciences and Engineering Research Council of Canada, the *Halifax Herald Limited*, Atlantic Television Systems, Baton Broadcasting Inc., Maritime Telephone & Telegraph, Atlantic Canada Organization for Research Networking, and Sun Microsystems of Canada Limited for their support of this research project. In addition, we would like to thank Theo Chiasson for his design and development of the layout and viewing software for the prototype shown at the G7 Economic Summit.

References

1. Ashton, F., and G. Cruickshank. 1993. The newspaper of the future: A look beyond the front porch. In *Proceedings of the 14th National On-line Meeting*, 11-16.

2. Becker, D. 1994. UTF—An SGML standard for the news distribution industry. In *Proceedings of the RIAO '94 Conference*, 631-648.

3. Bender, W., H. Lie, J. Orwant, L. Teodosio, and N. Abramson. 1991. Newspace: mass media and personal computing. In *Proceedings of the Summer 1991 USENIX Conference*, 329-349.

4. Burkowski, F. J., C. R. Watters, and M. A. Shepherd. 1994a. Delivery of electronic news: A broadband application. In *Proceedings of CASCON '94* (CD-ROM).

5. ———. 1994b. "Electronic News Delivery." Technical Report PR-94-01, University of Waterloo, Dept. of Computer Science.

6. Ferguson, R. 1994. Info highway will soon travel almost anywhere. *The Chronicle-Herald*. April 22, p. B7.

7. Gladney, H. M., et al. 1994. Digital library: Gross structure and requirements: Report from a March 1994 workshop. In *Proceedings of Digital Libraries '94*, 101-107.

8. Newspaper Association of America. 1994. *IPTC-NAA Universal Text Format*, 0.8 edition.

9. Noras, S. R. 1989. All the news that's fit to screen—the development of fulltext newspaper databases. *Australian Library Journal*, 38:17-27.

10. Pack, T. 1993. Electronic newspapers—the state of the art. In *Proceedings of the 14th National Online Meeting*, 331-335.

11. Putz, W., and E. J. Neuhold. 1991. is-News: a multimedia information system. *IEEE Data Engineering*, 14:16-25.

12. Shepherd, M. A., C. R. Watters, and F. J. Burkowski. 1995a. Delivery of electronic news. In *The Second International Workshop on Next Generation Information Technologies and Systems*, 124-131.

13. ———. 1995b. Digital libraries for electronic news. In *Advances in Digital Libraries*, 13-20.

Chapter 7

Electronic Publishing in a University Setting: The Centralization vs. Decentralization Debate

Mary M. LaMarca
Dartmouth College*

Abstract

In their efforts to maintain effective electronic publishing infrastructures, such as Campus Wide Information Systems, universities have once again been plunged into a familiar problem in organizational design: whether to centralize or decentralize. Unfortunately the debate—and the resulting decisions—have too often been dominated by "political" considerations and folklore about organizational efficiency, rather than an informed concern with maximizing overall institutional effectiveness.

This chapter considers the relevance of classic organizational theories to the centralization/decentralization issue in university electronic publishing. The general characteristics of electronic publishing in a university setting are laid out. An overview of general organizational theory with respect to centralization/decentralization follows. The chapter then examines two representative electronic publishing cases at Brown University, its Campus Wide Information System (CWIS), a gopher-based system, and its World Wide Web (WWW). The effects of centralization/decentralization on university electronic publishing are examined. Finally, a set of recommendations is outlined for the organization of electronic publishing in a university setting.

Introduction

During the last few years, universities have been wrestling with how to distribute information on campus electronically. They have developed Campus

81

Wide Information Systems (CWIS), and have experimented with a number of technologies—from FTP sites to gopher-based systems to the World Wide Web (WWW). A common problem runs through all these technological advances: how does this online information stay current and relevant to the community?

The problem creates tension between the information services staff and the information publishers on the campus. Computing and information services develop and test the network infrastructure and some have initiated and supported pilot electronic publishing projects on campus. They feel that they have proven the infrastructure and applications work, and now want the information providers to publish and maintain their own data. But information providers at a university are a diverse lot—they include academic and administrative departments, faculty, the library, and university relations. The providers realize they should publish their information on the network, but they are not eager to learn the technical skills necessary to format the information for publishing.

At Brown University, we are attempting to work out the relationship between the role of the individual information provider and the role of the university as publisher. Should electronic publishing be viewed as an extension to traditional publishing and come under the control of a centralized department such as University Relations? This department traditionally controls the image of the university, it tends to standardize publications and market the university in a consistent way. Or should electronic publishing on campus follow the "anything goes" philosophy of the Internet and allow any and all forms of publication to exist under the aegis of the university? Should a university maintain a central communications/information office to which departments can send their information for formatting and editing? Is one central office with publication experts more efficient than distributing the publication process throughout the campus?

General Characteristics of University Electronic Publishing

In this chapter, the term "electronic publishing" is roughly defined as any way of making information available in electronic form using computers and computer networks. This is somewhat broader than the more common definition, which is to recreate some type of printed journal by duplicating or processing it electronically. Electronic publishing can be made available to the worldwide community via global networks like the Internet. Some examples of electronic publishing technology relevant in a university setting are Gopher, WAIS, World Wide Web, listservs, newsgroups, ftp servers, and file servers.

---

* The author worked at Brown University, Computing and Information Services from September 1989 through February 1996 as a Senior Consultant/Analyst. She is currently the Assistant Director of Information Systems at Dartmouth College.

This chapter deals specifically with two types of electronic publishing at Brown, the Campus Wide Information System (CWIS), a gopher-based publishing system and the World Wide Web (WWW).

Electronic publishing in an academic setting involves a wide range of patterns and types of information. For example:

- University Relations would like to publish its weekly staff newspaper and press releases to the Internet
- Academic and administrative departments want to publish their hours of operation and their staff listings
- The library wants to publish directions for access to its electronic resources, pointers to other information services on the Internet, and databases of special collections
- Faculty members want to publish course-related materials, such as syllabi and laboratory instructions; they also want to communicate electronically with their students and to publish student research
- Student groups would like to advertise their organizations and publish schedules of activities
- Human Resources wants to publish policy manuals and university guidelines electronically so they do not have to print out individual copies for every staff person on campus.

Each of these publishing examples has a specific purpose; they fall under the category of either traditional institutional publishing (Human Resources Policy Manual), curricular use (syllabi), marketing (press releases), or location of bibliographic material (library special collections). The staff members involved in electronic publishing basically assume the same roles as those in traditional publishing. These jobs include the author or information provider who creates the information; the editor who organizes or refines the information; and the service operator who prepares the information for publication. The users, of course, are the same regardless of the publishing method.

Electronic publishing on a campus is primarily used for information dissemination, and support of research and instruction. It is an excellent way to take advantage of the campus network infrastructure that has been created during the past decade. It is possible to create a coherent electronic campus-wide system to support learning and research. Incoming students are beginning to demand these new electronic services, and it is crucial that the university supply them with the requested information in the most efficient way possible.

Our experience at Brown University with both the gopher-based CWIS and the WWW reveals that many departments wish to publish administrative information about their activities; electronic publishing seems to be viewed as a marketing tool to inform users about a specific department. Until recently, we had not found many faculty members who wanted to publish traditional academic information, such as their research or databases of subject-based information. Now we find that attitudes are changing rapidly. The use of peer-reviewed electronic journals is slowly being accepted throughout the academic community. Faculty members are beginning to experiment with publishing their research and interests on the Internet: it enables them to easily share information with their colleagues at other institutions.

For a publication to be useful, whether generated on paper or electronically, it must have accurate information and be relevant to its audience. Individual departments are most likely to know the type of information their users need, therefore a department is best positioned to create and distribute publications on an "as-needed" basis.

Most traditional university publications—e.g., course listings, telephone books, handbooks, policy manuals—are compilations of information generated by multiple providers; a majority are at the departmental level. Usually a designated person, such as a departmental administrative assistant, coordinates and collects the information. Furthermore, most university information is dynamic: instructors and class information change from semester to semester; housing and phone numbers change as well. This brings up the issue of the currency of information. Users of print publications produced once a year do not expect the information to be current throughout the year; however, the same is not true of electronic publications—users expect those to remain current since they assume a central entity in charge of electronic information will update it whenever necessary.

Centralization/Decentralization/Organizational Theory

Centralization and decentralization describe ways in which decision making is dispersed or delegated in an organizational hierarchy. Central administration may have decision making power over subunits which often lie within different geographical areas, and possibly on different hierarchical levels from the central administration. Centralization/decentralization deals with the problem of the whole and individual parts and how decision making authority is distributed over these parts. It is difficult to measure centralization and decentralization in an organization, and it is difficult to make comparisons over time and between organizations due to their complexity.

Every organizational system falls somewhere on the centralization/decentralization continuum, with a healthy functioning combination of the two. According to the *International Encyclopedia of the Social Sciences*, no true totally centralized system and no true totally decentralized system exist. A completely centralized organizational system would have all decision making authority at the highest level, while a completely decentralized system would have every person in an organization sharing equally in the decision making authority. A system operating at either of these extremes would result in anarchy (Lynch 1989).

A romantic ideal of decentralization seems to exist; apparently related to the ideal of democracy—if every individual makes his/her own decisions, then each decision must be the best for the whole. It is almost as if decentralization has been transformed into a value in its own right (Fesler 1965). Centralization is so out of current favor that there is a tendency to take for granted when a department is accountable and responsive to local conditions that it is a natural outcome of decentralization—though this has never been proven. This belief leads to a general dismissal of the possibility that a strong central decision making authority might benefit local departments.

Standard organizational theory suggests that as units within a system are more dispersed geographically, and acquire more specialization and distinction from the central division, the communication, control and coordination between unit and central division becomes more difficult (Alexander and Fennell 1986). The paradox of organizational theory is that successful decentralization depends on strong centralization. Strong central leadership, which combines a strong sense of purpose with an effective strategy and structure, is essential for successful decentralization. The optimum organization is a dynamic system that balances the benefits of local administration autonomy with the pursuit of unified central goals. In addition the central system and subunits help each other understand their responsibilities, limitations, and prerogatives (Murphy 1989). Good communication is essential in a well-run organizational system.

Service organizations, such as governments, hospitals, and universities, are complex. Nonetheless, we can make a number of basic assumptions about them: units within these systems tend to be dispersed geographically; the primary function, and goals of one unit may differ from another; decision making within a unit may be different from another unit; and some units will operate more efficiently and much more autonomously than others.

It is important to be able to see decisions about management of resources and electronic publishing services in this light. Our experience at Brown with CWIS and WWW are very good case studies of this problem.

Specific Examples of University Electronic Publishing

Gopher Implementation

In 1992, Computing and Information Services (CIS) and the Brown Library implemented a gopher-based campus wide information system (CWIS). We faced the classic chicken and egg problem. We needed enough information so that users would want to use the new service, but it was difficult to persuade departments to give us information until they felt that people would want to use it.

In order to make the CWIS a useful system, we approached a number of information-rich administrative departments on campus. Initial information for the CWIS was provided by CIS, the Brown News Bureau, the Dean of the College's office, the Registrar, the library, Human Resources, and the Office of Student Life. We created relevant local area information by soliciting information from the Rhode Island Department of Tourism and by providing local transportation schedules. The library and CIS purchased Clarinet, an online news service, which we included in the CWIS. We also created gateways to enable gopher users to access some of our other campus-based systems, enabling users to access and search the "Brown Online Course Announcements", "Brown Job Listings", the "Electronic Address Book," and "Josiah," our library catalog, directly from the CWIS.

For the CWIS, we decided to institute a system of distributed information providers. Each department created and maintained its own information, assuming the roles of information provider and editor. The department decided what information was most relevant, and then either converted existing publications to electronic format or created new information for inclusion on the CWIS. Training was provided on good organizational practices and file naming conventions, then the departments determined the menu structure and file names for their own information. Some departments also contributed to the service operator role and formatted their information for the CWIS. They then turned it over to a central administrator who executed the final service operator role and physically moved the information to the CWIS. A central administration team, composed of staff members from the library and CIS, maintained the general organizational structure of the CWIS and cross-linked relevant pieces of information.

We established a group of approximately 75 users, from both academic and administrative departments, to test our new system for two months. During our user feedback sessions, the following items were raised as the most important:

- users perceived that a central department was in charge of the information on the CWIS
- users wanted information to be up-to-date and accurate
- users were frustrated by empty folders and dead-ends
- users wanted simpler menu organization
- users wanted more searching capabilities.

We modified the standard gopher server to address some of the above items. To illustrate that no central department was in charge of the information, we added a "provider" field so that users would see the names and e-mail addresses of the information providers when they viewed a particular file. To indicate the relevancy and currency of information, we added "creation date" and "expiration date" fields. Through manipulation of the date, we also created a "What's new on the Brown CWIS?" function. This let a user easily discover the latest information added to the server. We also implemented an expiration procedure. The server would automatically remind information providers by e-mail at a set time that a document was about to expire, and the server removed the expired items if the providers did not update the information. The expiration process allowed us to control the currency of information by automatically removing the out-of-date information. We also revamped the main menu and eliminated empty folders and dead-ends. We added a "Search the Brown CWIS" to help users find their required information.

After two years of the CWIS pilot project, we discovered that despite our creation of useful maintenance tools, information providers were not able to maintain their own information. Once a document expired and was removed from the gopher, it was never replaced with a more up-to-date version. The departments kept their original organizational structure, and rarely added any new information to the gopher. Very few additional departments decided to contribute their information to the CWIS—a prime reason being that simple conversion tools did not exist for painless conversion of word processed documents. No usage statistics were generated to prove that users were accessing the information on the CWIS, therefore departments had no way of knowing whether their efforts were paying off. These negative factors combined to push electronic publishing of information to the bottom of departmental priorities.

In addition to lack of interest at the departmental level, a shift in priorities also occurred within CIS, the department that housed the central administration of the gopher. The overhead involved in maintaining and modifying a nonstandard gopher server caused incompatibility problems, it was difficult to modify the server for updates and new features. CIS is in the process of converting the gopher server to the standard gopher-plus protocol, thus removing many of our specialized modifications.

We plan to hand over the information update process to the information providers and not maintain a central administrator to coordinate activity. Information providers will obtain a userid on a UNIX box, be assigned a hierarchical space on the gopher server, and be responsible for transferring and keeping their information up to date on the server. In the future, a department will assume all the publishing roles: author, editor, service provider and user. The only central service the university will provide is storage space on a central server, and maintenance of the overall organizational structure of the CWIS. There will be no provider training, or automatic expiration procedures. I foresee that this situation will quickly cause the CWIS to be filled with information that is out of date and inaccurate.

WWW Implementation

Some departments are more technologically literate than others; for example, science departments have traditionally implemented "bleeding-edge" technologies as soon as they become available. In 1993, a number of the science departments began to set up WWW servers and publish home pages for their departments. One department even went so far as to set up a central university home page. At the same time, a student group set up a file server and advertised to the campus that it was willing to publish Web pages. This combination of factors caused us to shift focus from gopher technology toward working with the WWW. We now organize and maintain the central home page, and have implemented a university-wide method for publishing information to the Web. After our experience with the gopher server, instead of going out and recruiting information providers we decided to set a process in place such that motivated departments or groups could publish information to the Web. We implemented this service in October 1994. A central administrator in CIS maintains the Brown WWW home page. When a department has created its home page, it e-mails the Webmaster, who then links the department's home page to the Brown home page.

Our brief experience with the Brown WWW publishing service leads us to the following conclusions. Academic departments, especially the more technically advanced departments, are taking advantage of the service. The student organizations that have published on the Web have at least one motivated student who is interested in learning about the WWW and HTML. There also tends to be some competition between the student groups—every single music-based student organization has created a Web page. On the other hand, none of the "critical" information providers on campus, such as the Registrar or the Office of Student Life, is interested in publishing on the Web. These administrative departments tend to operate under pressure and be short on staff during most of the year; they do not seem willing to put time and effort into learning a new system, especially after their recent and inconclusive experiment with gopher technology.

Though we consider the WWW to be just another example of electronic publishing on the campus—even an extension to the CWIS—we find that users perceive it quite differently. Since many more academic departments are publishing to the Web, it seems to be perceived as a more "serious" and scholarly system.

Information providers are much more concerned about where their information appears on the Brown home page, and how they are perceived in the university's hierarchy. Inclusion on the Brown home page has become politicized and much more significant to departments. Because faculty take it more seriously, we are finding that senior administration is beginning to view electronic publishing on campus as an important tool.

University Electronic Publishing and Organizational Theory

If we view a university's business as the creation, processing, and dissemination of information (Langenberg 1994), then electronic publishing—which by definition also involves the creation, processing, and dissemination of information—should be viewed as an integral part of a university's way of doing business and deployed as widely as possible. A university could decide to centralize electronic publishing. In this case, a central group reporting to a senior administrative officer or board might function as a publishing center. Possibly a group such as University Relations could act as this publishing center. It could create a set of standards to which each department must adhere, and require each department to publish electronically. This would allow for the marketing of the university in a consistent way. This central group should decide on the information that the campus needs to run more efficiently, compile it, and publish it. This option would likely cost more than other methods, but could prove more effective in the long run.

Another option the university might take is a "do-it-yourself" approach to electronic publishing. This option tends to favor decentralization. This would not cost any real money up front; each department would be empowered to make its own electronic publishing decisions. Organizational research shows it as a given that departments will be accountable for their information and will be responsive to their users needs. Our CWIS experience has proven otherwise: departments were empowered to maintain their electronic publishing information, but they failed to keep information current, therefore not reacting to their users needs.

As people and money resources become tighter, and the trend continues towards the decentralization of technology and the distribution of publishing to subunits, some undesirable trends begin to appear. In some cases, departmental publishing may increase, but at the sacrifice of expertise, group efficiency and the viewpoint of the whole organization (Gilette 1989). Each department will have to employ a different individual for the task of electronic publishing. No overall vision guides the university and each department acts as an independent agent. This scenario brings up the quality problem, because when each department publishes separately, no standards exist. Some departments will publish, some will not; some will publish in a slipshod fashion, and some will devote money and energy to the process.

Some departments will view electronic publishing as an opportunity for innovation, using the current technology to its full potential. The heads of those departments realize that they own the information and are interested in becoming partners in its further development; they are willing to take on the responsibility of becoming information managers (Bloomfield and Coombs 1992). In the electronic publishing arena, this will mean dedicating some of their employees to learning and implementing the new publishing technologies (such as HTML). Using individuals in that way naturally impacts departmental time and money. The department head must be sufficiently confident that a foray into electronic technology will eventually pay off.

On the other hand, some departments will view electronic publishing as change beyond their control. These departments will tend to be small, lacking the people, time, or energy to devote to the new technologies. They will not participate unless directed to do so by the central administration (Gilette 1989).

Recommendations for Electronic Publishing in a University Setting

There are no clear-cut answers as to how electronic publishing should be handled in a university setting. Our experience at Brown with the CWIS and WWW shows that we need to find the right combination of centralized and decentralized control over management of electronic publishing services:

- the central administration of the university needs to agree that electronic publishing is a mission critical activity of the university
- a center for the handling of electronic publishing should be established to coordinate and deal with university electronic publishing, developing central information services to benefit the university community
- departments should be empowered to create the information they feel their users need
- publishers should be provided with guidelines concerning which information is essential for electronic publication
- all aspects of electronic publishing should be made as simple as possible for the publisher.

Coherent Administrative Philosophy

The manner in which information technology is applied ultimately becomes an issue of administrative philosophy. Due to a high degree of decentralization,

90

universities have been described in literature as "organized anarchies" (Simsek and Louis 1994). This tradition of decentralization in universities, with academic units making decisions independent not only of each other but quite often of the central administration, makes it essential for senior administration to define how information technology, specifically electronic publishing, is used on campus. "There is an ongoing need for service to individual users and the need for leadership in integrating technology and learning." (Langenberg 1994) New technologies, such as WWW, make this integration of technology and learning a reality. One just has to look at how some of the more technically sophisticated academic departments now are making use of this publishing technology in order to see its future possibilities for the whole campus.

As research has proven in successful decentralized systems, it is necessary that a university's leaders define a campus-wide electronic publishing direction. Because universities are so decentralized, a strong and coherent philosophy on electronic publishing is crucial. The university must decide on how electronic publishing should be used on campus and set guidelines to achieve that vision. This might be done by dictating that all departments use electronic publishing for information distribution.

Create a Central University Electronic Publishing Center

The growing reliance on information technology for decision making and delivery of services makes electronic publishing an extremely relevant issue in the centralization debate. Technology can be viewed as an event that triggers social changes, which effect how organizations operate. Sometimes technological change happens so fast that decisions about the use of information technology evolve almost by default. It may be necessary to formalize a structure to facilitate adoption of a new technology, such as electronic publishing, by creating new rules, norms, and roles.

To facilitate adoption of electronic publishing, we recommend the creation of a university-wide electronic publishing center. This center would have a variety of charges. Perhaps foremost would be to create a unified electronic campus-wide information system for use within and outside the university. The center should also provide a single point of contact for electronic publishing customers, staffed with people who are familiar with current electronic publishing technologies and able to gain competence quickly with emerging technologies. The staff members will understand the electronic publishing process and support knowledge work. They will use advanced hardware and software, and if appropriate develop a charge-back system that will reflect the efficiency and quality advantages of having production experts do the work.

All efforts should be made to keep costs as low as possible. The electronic publishing center will train and assist in manuscript preparation, create standards for publishing, provide guidance in locating or creating electronic repositories of texts, and help with copyright clearance issues. The center will provide space on a server to publish material, and will support a production-based server for the published material (James 1989). Electronic publishing of information and the maintenance of the information needs to become simpler. The electronic publishing center should investigate new technologies for the maintenance and publication of university information.

In our initial gopher beta test, we discovered that users already perceived that a central department was administrating and maintaining the CWIS information. This belief exists because the CWIS project was implemented by CIS and announced by CIS, a department that many users on campus believe is working under the direction of central university administration. Users' belief that a central department is in charge of information allows the electronic publishing center to act as that central department.

Through their contacts with the user community, the electronic publishing center can determine the types of services that the campus requires. These services should have up-to-date dynamic information that is relevant to the university community. The electronic publishing center can coordinate the information from the various information owners and assemble it into a coherent system for use. Types of central information services include online course information, online phone books, online events for the campus, and conversion of current paper-based published materials into electronic form. Electronic access to these new services will benefit the community by allowing access at all times by everyone in the university. These services can range from simple information such as local public transportation schedules to resource schedulers for the campus.

Empower Departments to Become Information Publishers

Many departments and faculty members on campus are interested in publishing information electronically. If a department is sufficiently large and technologically advanced, it likely has already attempted electronic publishing. The departments that are small and understaffed are the ones that need to be targeted. Communicate to these departments that publishing information electronically is a worthwhile goal, then help them reach that goal by supplying the requisite resources—human and technological. Create guidelines that specify the information essential for electronic publication. Staff members from the central university electronic publishing center can individually help these departments collate and publish their information.

After the essential university information is published, each department understands best the additional information their users need. The electronic publishing center can help these departments to publish their specialized information. It is also imperative that the published information remain accurate. Guidance for the departments must include procedures and processes to keep the information as up-to-date as possible, and this maintenance must be done at a departmental level.

Summary

As organizational theory suggests, at any given time both centralization and decentralization coexist in a system. During the initial development of the Brown CWIS, we created a loosely centralized electronic publishing strategy. We attempted to create a CWIS system by convincing departments to contribute to a centrally maintained system. We discovered that users assumed that CIS was in charge of the information since we maintained the server and was the system's primary service operator. Any information to be included in the Brown CWIS had to be passed to us for inclusion. Our campus-wide WWW publishing structure is primarily decentralized. We are turning control of the information to each department and hoping that they consider it important enough to devote time and resources into developing and maintaining their departmental information electronically. Our electronic publishing structure is evolving over time, and we continue to study the alternatives and expect to create a healthy combination of centralized and decentralized publishing strategies in the future.

In order for electronic publishing to be successful at a university, strong central leadership must decide that electronic publishing is an integral part of a university. The leadership must then create a strategy and structure for this mission and communicate its worth to all departments on the campus. Without this combination of strong, decisive leadership and a demonstrated sense of purpose, the trend towards decentralization of electronic publishing is bound for failure.

References

Alexander, J. C., and M. L. Fennell. 1986. Patterns of Decision Making in Multihospital Systems. *Journal of Health and Social Behavior*, 27(1), 14-27.

Bloomfield, B. P., and R. Coombs. 1992. Information technology, control and power: the centralization and decentralization debate revisited. *Journal of Management Studies*, 29(4), 459-484.

Fesler, J. W. 1965. Approaches to the Understanding of Decentralization. *The Journal of Politics*, 27, 536-566.

Gilette, J. E. 1989. Electronic Publishing: Trends and Responsive Strategies. *Book Research Quarterly*, 5(1, Spring), 10-19.

James, T. K. 1989. The Impact of Electronic Publishing Systems: An Organizational Model for a New Way of Doing Business. *Book Research Quarterly*, 5(1), 20-23.

Langenberg, D. N. 1994. Information Technology and the University: Integration Strategies for the 21st Century. *Journal of the American Society for Information Science*, 45(5), 323-325.

Lynch, R. G. 1989. Centralization and decentralization redefined. *Journal of Comparative Economics*, 13(March), 1-14.

Murphy, J. T. 1989. The Paradox of Decentralizing Schools: Lessons from Business, Government, and the Catholic Church. *Phi Delta Kappa*, 70(10), 808-812.

Simsek, H., and K. S. Louis. 1994. Organizational change as paradigm shift: Analysis of the change process in a large public university. *Journal of Higher Education*, 65(6), 670-695.

Chapter 8

HortBase: An Example of Professional Societies' Roles in Electronic Information Systems

John C. Matylonek
Oregon State University

James L. Green
Oregon State University

Evelyn Liss
Oregon State University

Andy Duncan
Oregon State University

Abstract

HortBase is a proposal for a peer-reviewed, synthesized electronic information system for storage-diffusion of agricultural information used in the classroom, in distance education, in lifelong learning, and in commercial agriculture production. It is a proposal to maintain (1) the roles and activities of the agricultural production, communication, and information science (library) faculty who currently create and distribute educational information, (2) the role of national academic discipline societies who verify quality of information in their respective academic disciplines through peer review, and (3) the role of national organizations such as the USDA-CSREES (Cooperative State Research, Education and Extension Service), the Coalition for Networked Information (CNI), and the National Agricultural Library (NAL) in providing guidelines, standards, and support on a national level. HortBase will be one of several networks within the proposed Agricultural Network Alliance (ANA) coordinated by AgNIC, the Agricultural Network Information Center (Figure 8.1).

Introduction

This proposal is innovative because it includes national peer review of synthesized extension and educational information similar to peer review applied primarily to reports of original research. It is a new proposal because it calls for national coordination and distribution of the workload and costs involved in

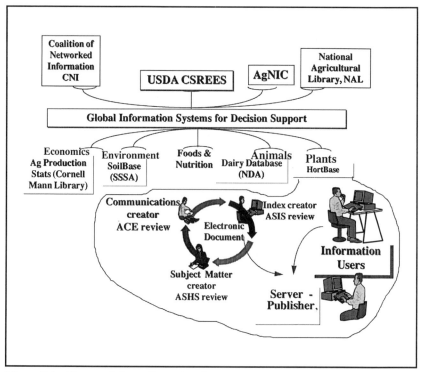

Figure 8.1: Proposed three-dimensional team creation-review of the GISDS files is illustrated under HortBase. Files will be created by three-dimensional teams (subject, communications, and information science team members). The dimension contributed by each of the respective team members will be reviewed by their respective national professional society.

creation, review/revision, and diffusion of the electronic information. This project aims to work within currently accepted standards of open systems design. Given the lack of standards for peer reviewed communication systems, however, it will advocate the creation of technological standards among academic computer system professionals and their faculty associates. It is a radical proposal because it calls for team creation of the electronic information files—a subject author, a communications specialist, and an information science faculty—working together to outline the file and to create it. The capabilities of the electronic information systems facilitate, indeed require, this new approach to information development and delivery.

For several years, James Green has worked at the grass roots and at the national level to conceptualize a USDA-CSREES Global Information System for Decision Support (GISDS) with horticulture as a pilot program. The American

Society for Horticultural Science (ASHS) Board at its annual meeting, August 11, 1994, unanimously recommended that the ASHS Extension vice president (Green) work to form an alliance among the USDA Extension Service, the USDA National Agricultural Library, the ASHS and other appropriate groups to develop HortBase as a pilot program. HortBase is to be presented at the ASHS annual meetings in Lexington, Kentucky, on October 7, 1996. The pilot program will be designed on a matrix to display horticulture topics in a range of electronic media (e.g., text, slides/illustrations, video, multimedia).

The HortBase pilot program is a prototype for other networks within the proposed GISDS. Responsibility for creating "chunks" or files of specific, concise information (Boeri and Hensel 1996) on agricultural subjects can be distributed nationwide among production teams comprised of agricultural extension-education subject, communication, and library faculty at land grant universities. This approach centers the author, review, and information diffusion system network with the national/international academic societies and their members rather than at the universities and their individual faculty level. This transcends university and geographical boundaries by forming virtual production and review "dream teams." Production team members may be at diverse geographical locations, but they work as a virtual team through electronic communication.

Nationwide teams of subject matter faculty, in cooperation with communication and library science collaborators, will be responsible for authoring and maintaining the peer reviewed, public access information files they have elected to create. National distribution of the array of information topics to respective teams for their creation is less redundant and more efficient than having faculty at each institution independently creating *all* of these extensive, wide ranging information files for use solely within their respective states.

By distributing the responsibility for information synthesis and maintenance for only a small portion of the total files to each team, individual faculty members will have more time for assisting clientele in identifying the "questions" and retrieving information from the national HortBase that is specific to their needs. Rather than spending their time finding and transferring information, faculty will have more time to interact with the information users (students, Extension clientele, etc.). Faculty can become *coaches*, rather than lecturers. "Teachers are coming out from behind their lecture podiums to interact more with their students . . . deploying new high-tech tools to reach their students, ranging from using computers to help them visualize the abstract laws of physics to performing chemistry experiments on their computer screens. But as much fun as these new tools are to use, they're no substitute for a faculty member's presence in the laboratory or the lecture room." (Gibbons 1994)

The lines are blurring among information used in life-long learning, extension education, extended or distance education, and on-campus education as we become information synthesizers. Cetron and Davies (1994) say that "individuals will learn more on their own, the 'places' of learning will be more dispersed, and the age at which things are learned will depend on individual ability, not tradition. Education is becoming more individualized as interactive computer/videodisk systems and other new media permit students to learn according to their needs and abilities. Personal computers with ultra-high resolution screens, 3-D graphics, high-level interactivity, artificial intelligence, and virtual reality will enhance gaming and simulations (e.g., cases studies) used in education and training. Corporations now invest some $85 billion per year in employee education and retraining. That will double by 2001."

We envision that primary authors/reviewers of the public accessible HortBase files will be both extension and resident instruction faculty. Extension and education faculty will be both file creators and file users. In discussing the ideas with Oregon State University (OSU) Department of Horticulture faculty who are primarily in education (resident instruction, continuing education and Extension), they see real benefits to faculty, students, and the general public. Faculty could be authors on nationally peer reviewed files, e.g., greenhouse covering materials, tissue culture propagation of specific plants, etc. And information content would be current in the maintained up-to-date files. Students and other users could access the electronic information system to explore special interests, to research assignments, or for review. If quality horticultural instructional information is readily available, the total quality of K-16, extended education, and lifelong learning will be enhanced.

The Agricultural Electronic Information System

We propose to develop, maintain and distribute the electronic information files through the steps delineated in Figure 8.1 and detailed in the following text.

Creation, Review, Revision,
Maintenance of Network Information Files

Creation. Subject matter faculty are members of the file creation team. Each individual member will assume primary responsibility to author and maintain a discrete, reasonable number of files on the national electronic information system. For example, a faculty member in the OSU Department of Horticulture might be the primary author on blueberry production or on a few specific aspects of blueberry production such as pruning. The author's national peers, say in New England and Georgia, would review the production information for completeness and accuracy. Because of the new and expanded characteristics of electronic information systems, however, the files will not be created by the subject matter faculty alone. Each file creation team will have three members: subject matter, communications, and information management.

Communication faculty are co-creators. "The hardest topics for me to get across are the things that I can see in my head that the students don't have a clue about," says chemist Nathan Lewis of the California Institute of Technology. "We want to put those things on screen for them." Lewis' efforts involve a team of animators led by a Hollywood special effects producer. The 10-minute videos show complex processes in 3-D; at the end of the $2-million project "you'll be able to watch atomic orbitals dance with Jurassic Park-style." (Culotta, 1994) The communication faculty member(s) of the team will assist in communicating the information to the target audience by selecting appropriate media, information sequence, electronic document design.

Library faculty specializing in electronic storage, search, retrieval, and distribution of electronic information are members of the file creation teams. The files will be designed from the beginning to facilitate indexing, archiving, and distribution of the electronic information. Design is integrated from the beginning and throughout the information file creation as compared to cataloging, and possibly required redesign, of the completed subject document. Alternate players in this role may be content oriented systems professionals or agriculture faculty interested in knowledge management.

Concurrent, rather than sequential input into file development by the subject, library, and communication faculty will create a unified electronic publication. Subject authors will develop concise, easily indexed and retrieved "chunks" of specific information, rather than books, chapters, or paragraphs. Communication faculty will develop illustrations and document design to ensure rapid retrieval, searching, and distribution of the information file. Library faculty will work closely with subject and communication faculty from the initiation of the file creation.

Daniel E. Atkins, dean of the School of Information and Library Studies at the University of Michigan envisions that the new librarian "will combine the skills of the computer scientist, the business graduate and even a little of the old-school librarian . . . to help make sense of the labyrinth of different information sources available on the Internet. You can waste 24 hours a day browsing." (Stix, 1994) Rather than waiting for a labyrinth to develop, in our proposal the library faculty will be co-creating the files and making sense of the information files *before* they are on the Internet.

Like the subject matter and communication workload, the "library" workload also would be distributed nationally. Each cooperating library or faculty member likely would specialize in one or more groups of topics, subjects, or technology information. For example, the information management faculty at the Oregon State University Kerr Library might catalog horticulture electronic information files, Purdue University's library might catalog agronomic crops, and the Mann Library at Cornell University might catalog agricultural production statistics. Because the information is in electronic form and readily transmitted on the Internet, national distribution and specialization can occur—the file creation team members do not need to be at the same geographical location. "Virtual teams" can be formed with subject matter, communications, and information management team members at diverse geographical sites.

Review. "Educators and publishers have started to worry about a time when the Internet might become clogged with programs that are mediocre or even worse, filled with inaccuracies." (Service 1994) Stix (1994) states that "some academics fear that the sheer volume of literature and a growing inability to distinguish the good from the bad in what gets published (on the Internet) may lead to an overall decline in standards."

After team creation of the file by the subject matter, communication, and library faculty, the file will be transmitted electronically to the team members' respective national societies for peer review of the subject matter (e.g., American Society for Horticultural Science), of the communications aspects (e.g., Agricultural Communicators in Education), and of the information management facets (e.g., American Society for Information Science). National peer review will not only validate and maintain the credibility of the files, it will also serve as continued education, development, networking, and peer recognition for the creators in their respective professional fields. Peer review will enhance widespread use of the information because of the "distributed ownership."

The structure for national peer review of the file's subject matter will be provided by the appropriate national academic societies. The national academic societies will be recognized for quality control; e.g., ASHS will be known publicly as "the source of validated horticulture information."

Revision. The reviewed files will be returned electronically through the national societies to the subject matter, communications, and information management creators for revision. Revised files will be returned to the national discipline society for diffusion to users/clients; e.g., horticulture subject-matter files will be returned to the ASHS HortBase network for public access.

Maintenance. Clifford Lynch, president of the American Society for Information Science (ASIS) and director of library automation at the University of California states that "scholarly and professional societies have missions and values highly consistent with mission and values of the library and higher education communities. A reaffirmation of these missions by the societies as part of the development of electronic publishing programs should play a vital role in rebuilding a sense of common cause with the university and research library worlds . . . ." (Lynch, 1994) Final drafts for HortBase will be electronically stored on servers maintained by library faculty within the Information Services arm of OSU. Because networks have only administrative limitations, not geographical ones, this role could be held by other units and individuals on campus. Given the opportunity of knowledge management administration within electronic publishing, however, it seems that Internet-oriented librarians are the best qualified and interested professionals within traditional university organizations.

Client Access/Service

To maintain local state identification and support, it may be desirable to have clients access the information through their respective land grant university's home page on the World Wide Web (WWW).

To maintain creator, validator identification, and support, specific information retrieved by clients will include a "tag line":

> Subj. Author_____, Comm. Author_____, Info. Syst.
> Author _____
> Reviewed/Approved by (academic societies, e.g., ASHS, ACE, or
> ASIS) on (date).

The respective subject networks (e.g., HortBase of the ASHS) of the USDA GISDS will have front-end query systems where clients can post questions for which they did not find answers on the network. These client-posted queries will trigger development of new information files by the network manager, e.g., ASHS, or be referred through AgNIC to the appropriate agricultural information network. Query-driven development of new files, continual revision and update of existing files, and deletion of unused files will ensure a user-responsive system.

Support

General guidelines and support, and software will be provided through USDA-CSREES to the subject networks of the GISDS. File review procedures and management of the network systems by the respective discipline societies (e.g. ASHS, HortBase) of the GISDS will be supported by USDA-CSREES.

The USDA-CSREES must play a critical role in establishing general guidelines, prioritization, and support. Many of the faculty members of the file creation teams are USDA-CSREES faculty (Figure 8.2). A National Information Initiatives (NII) program similar to the National Research Initiatives (NRI) program of the USDA Agricultural Experiment Stations could be developed by the USDA-CSREES to identify, prioritize, and create a nationwide competitive grant funding program to stimulate information file development. For example, more than $5 million was granted in 1995 by USDA-CSREES, CTDE, and

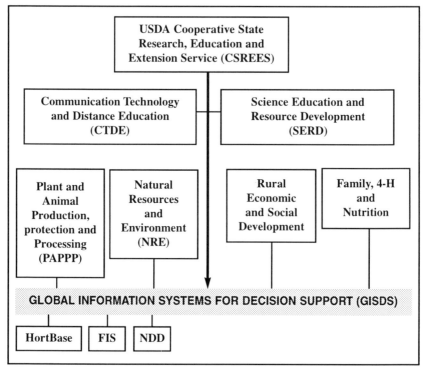

Figure 8.2: Organization flow chart within USDA-CSREES for GIDS funding and development; in 1995 CTDE and SERD provided more than $5 million as Challenge Grants for information development.

SERD for information development. Information faculty, like research faculty, also could submit proposals to other agencies and the private sector requesting funding for development of information files .

Who Will Pay?

Who pays for what is a crucial question. But, we first need to develop the system: what is needed, what is required to do it, and who would logically be doing it—then what will it cost? The proposed process (Figure 8.1) calls for national distribution of the workload among existing individual land grant university faculty and USDA employees who would develop their respective shares of the total electronic information system. Each individual faculty member would be developing fewer subject files and would have access to the remainder that are developed by colleagues at other sites.

In the proposed nationally distributed process, no more and possibly less faculty and dollars would be employed; and these would be used more efficiently by eliminating the current redundancy of many persons nationwide doing the same information development. The individual land grant university faculty will continue to have their salaries, operating dollars, and work times, but will redirect their resources to producing electronic information files rather than printed materials. It is a matter of transition from working with printed materials to working with electronic files.

Likewise, the national academic societies are currently publishing printed journals. The costs associated with the national peer review of the printed information and of publishing the journals are recovered by subscription fees. Similar user fees for access to the societies' electronic information network might be required. However Lynch (1994) observes that "there is no mandate within (professional societies) that a publication program be 'profitable.' At best, it may need to be self-supporting, in that a publication's program needs to be financed, either by direct revenue or from external sources such as membership dues." We would add that land grant institutions, agriculture extension programs, and libraries have the common goal of disseminating and effectively utilizing information, funds for which have been allocated based on a limited print production system.

By distributing the workload nationally and by forming alliances with the national academic societies, we will be able to do more with less.

Benefits to Society and Professional Members

Individual participants get definite benefits. Faculty of agriculture, communication, and libraries will increase their skills in which they develop networked scholarly resources within a peer reviewed protocol. Because the alliances formed increase the integrity and quality of information distribution and appropriate credit is established for the resources developed, these activities should be recognized by promotion and tenure committees. Concurrently, societies (such as ASIS) may recognize that members are creating technology standards for peer reviewed communication systems. The recognition and prestige of leading the higher level standards efforts addressing content and management will compliment the infrastructure standards for which the Internet Engineering Task Force and other bodies are responsible.

Societal Benefits and Compatibility With Societal Directions

Electronic information systems facilitate information transfer and learning through multimedia in ways previously not possible. Computer Technology Research (CTR) reports that people retain only twenty percent of what they see, thirty percent of what they hear, fifty percent of what they see and hear, and as much as eighty percent of what they simultaneously see, hear, and do (Hofstetter, 1994). Hofstetter (ibid) defines this active learning process as multimedia: "Multimedia is the use of a computer to present and combine text, graphics, audio, and video with links and tools that let the user navigate, interact, create, and communicate."

CTR estimates that the number of multimedia computers will grow by a compound average growth rate of 82 percent to 15.5 million systems in 1995. By 1998 the top applications will be entertainment ($9.1 billion), publishing ($4.7 billion), and education and training ($4.3 billion). The Universal Bi-directional Interactive Consortium of Quebec, Canada, has launched a $750-million electronic network eight-year project. With no hardware charge to consumers (charging only for services used), the first phase in 1995 offers direct debit home shopping and banking, e-mail, tutoring, etc. (Hofstetter, 1994).

Electronic communication technology and capabilities are introducing a new era. Creation, access, and interaction with electronic media can be distributed globally via the World Wide Web. The USDA-CSREES GISDS would be a likely "anchor" tenant on a major private or public network.

Many observers are concerned that citizens will not have hardware/software to access electronic information systems. Information can readily be converted downward from the higher technology format to the printed page for further distribution when desired. It is more difficult, however, to convert upward from the printed page to the electronic multimedia format. Our fear is not that potential users will be denied direct access to electronic information, but that access will occur before we can provide quality information, easily retrieved. "Once people realize that this technology has practical, helpful applications, I am confident they will embrace it and get connected." (Irving 1995)

Summary

By forming an alliance with other agencies and national societies to distribute the workload and costs of developing and maintaining a national electronic information service, the new technologies allow us to do more with less! We think the time is right for USDA-CSREES to develop the Global Information System for Decision Support.

References

Boeri, R.J. and Martin Hensel. 1996. Lost in Hypertext? Map your information! *CD-ROM Professional* April, 9 (4): 72-74.

Cetron, Marvin and Owen Davies. 1994. *The American renaissance in the year 2000—74 trends that will affect America's future—and yours.* Adapted from *Crystal Globe: The Haves and Have-Nots of the New World Order*, M.J. Cetron and O. Davies (Forecasting International, Ltd., 1001 North Highland Street, P.O. Box 1650, Arlington, VA 22201. Phone: 703-527-1311. fax: 703-527-0200), St. Martin's Press, 1991.

Culotta, E. 1994. New modes of making scientists. In: Science innovations on campus, edited by E. Rubenstein. *Science* 266:843-893, November.

Gibbons, A. 1994. Turning students on by simulating the arcane. In: Science innovations on campus, edited by E. Rubenstein. *Science* 266:843-893, November.

Hofstetter, Fred T. 1994. Is multimedia the next literacy? *Educators' Tech Exchange*, Winter 1994, 6-13.

Irving, Larry, U.S. Department of Commerce Assistant Secretary for Communications and Information. 1995. In: Clinton administration urges Americans to get connected to the information age, Release No. 0213.95 dated March 9, 1995, by Jim Desler, Paige Darden, Tom Amontree, and Jim Brownlee.

Lynch, C. A. 1994. Scholarly communication in the networked environment: reconsidering economics and organizational missions. *Serials Review* 20(3):23-30.

Service, R. F. 1994. Assault on the lesson plan. In: Science innovations on campus, edited by E. Rubenstein. *Science* 266:843-893, November.

Stix, Gary. 1994. The speed of write. *Scientific American* 271(6):106-111, December.

Chapter 9

Access to Electronic Information: A Comparative Evaluation

Stephen T. Bajjaly
University of South Carolina

Abstract

An empirical study comparing the usefulness of paper-based and electronic versions of the same document set was conducted by the Center for Technology in Government (CTG), located at the State University of New York at Albany. This study, one component of a broad examination of the costs and benefits associated with providing electronic access to government information, was designed to test whether online availability of policy documents is an acceptable, or even preferable, substitute for indexed access to their printed counterparts. This chapter presents an overview of the study's genesis, its methodology, and the results.

Background

An emerging trend in the 1990s is for public agencies at all levels to improve access to the vast storehouse of government information through the increased use of information technology systems. While computer networks and database systems produce unprecedented quantities of electronic information, an equally significant and, in fact, larger volume of government data remains paper bound. Printed documents remain inaccessible because their contents are known only through the fallible memories of a dispersed work force charged with a variety of separate, information-related tasks. While most public officials acknowledge their responsibility for sound record management practices and to provide public access to documents, they also point out that no resources are allocated directly to these functions; consequently, they receive low priority.

The State University of New York (SUNY), the largest university system in the world, encompasses sixty-four campuses spread across New York State. These campuses range from two-year community colleges and agricultural/technical colleges to four-year undergraduate and Ph.D. granting university centers. Each campus, relatively autonomous on day-to-day and procedural issues, interacts with SUNY Central Administration to develop and implement long-range, strategic plans and policies. The SUNY Board of Trustees, administratively based within SUNY Central, oversees the entire system and acts as the interface between the agency, the governor and the state legislature on higher education issues.

Over the past twenty years the SUNY Board has issued a number of relatively unstructured policy memoranda to the campus presidents on a variety of broadly based issues such as affirmative action, faculty research, and acceptable programs of study. An extremely limited number of copies of each memorandum has been distributed to offices in SUNY Central and to each campus president. An index to these memoranda was produced but, at the time of the study, had not been kept current for ten years. Recognizing that updating the index would be labor intensive and time consuming, it was decided to determine whether advances in relevant technology—document imaging and full-text retrieval—would not only eliminate the need for an index but actually improve overall access to and utility of the policy memoranda.

The Study

The "SuperBook Project," as it came to be known, was a partnership between SUNY Central, CTG, and two technology vendors, Bellcore Laboratories and Digital Equipment Corporation. SuperBook is client-server, full-text retrieval software with hypertext capabilities, developed at Bellcore Laboratories[1] (the research consortium of the Regional Bell Operating Companies). Digital provided the UNIX workstation used as the SuperBook server.

Phase I

Phase I activities included selection of appropriate policy memoranda to include in the study as well as installation and testing of the SuperBook system. From the total of more than 1500 pages of policy documents, it was decided to include 85 documents (500 pages). As none of these memoranda was available in machine-readable format, document scanning and conversion to plain, ASCII text were necessary preparatory activities. Due to the unstructured nature of the memoranda, as well as their inclusion of numerous logos, signatures, tables, etc., the conversion from paper to electronic format was a large and time consuming task.[2]

In addition to document conversion and clean-up activities, which were accomplished by members of the clerical staff, project staff members performed value-added activities to make the documents amenable to an electronic format. For example, phrases such as "attached," and "on the next page . . ." as well as page headers and footers (irrelevant in electronic documents that have no page distinctions) were minimized.

As an early client-server application, the project required significant testing to make SuperBook functional across both text-based and a variety of graphical front ends (e.g., UNIX, Windows, and Macintosh). Also, the software was still undergoing beta testing and tended to "crash" more than one would expect or tolerate in a production quality application. Nonetheless, despite the significant expenditure of personal resources on Phase I activities, its sponsors concluded that the technology appeared attractive, particularly for information dissemination activities, and warranted further investigation.

Phase II

Phase II activities encompassed the empirical tests and data analyses comparing users' ability to answer policy-related questions and satisfaction between computer-based and paper-based versions of the same documents.

Methodology. The SUNY Central staff developed six questions based on the policy memoranda. Of these, they determined two to be easy, two of medium difficulty, and two judged hard to answer. The empirical tests involved two sessions—one using paper and one using SuperBook. Each subject answered three questions (one easy, one medium, and one hard) during each test session. Subjects were randomly assigned to slots arranged by (1) the order in which the questions were presented and (2) whether the subject would start with SuperBook or with paper. After a 30-minute orientation to the SuperBook software, subjects were divided into two groups—one group starting with SuperBook and the other group moving to a different test room to begin with paper.[3]

Subjects were given ten minutes to answer each question and were asked to indicate where in the 500 pages of policy memoranda the answer was located. Of the 31 subjects in the study, almost all were SUNY Central employees, representing a variety of divisions, who volunteered to participate. Most subjects appeared familiar with the paper versions of the documents—some, in fact, seemed to almost know by heart which policies covered particular topics.

Analysis. The correct analysis for these data is complicated: as repeated measures of categorical data, the methodology is not widely known even among professional statisticians. Nevertheless, the methodology is a fairly standard PROC CATMOD in SAS, with each observation consisting of six questions, each with two response levels (correct, incorrect). This results in 64 (2^6) possible response combinations. Statisticians, however, rarely model response combinations. Instead, marginal probabilities, such as the proportion of subjects who correctly answered Question 3, are employed. With a relatively small number of marginal probabilities, this procedure is also useful for sparse data sets.

Subjects were tested in two blocks. In Block 1, subjects answered Questions 1, 2, and 3 with SuperBook; Questions 4, 5, and 6 with paper. In block 2, subjects answered Questions 1, 2, and 3 with paper; Questions 4, 5, and 6 with SuperBook. If the marginal probabilities pattern differs between the blocks, the questions would not be homogeneous. In this case, the analysis of variance was not significant and, therefore, the blocks proved homogeneous.

The general SAS model tests the marginal probability of obtaining a given score on a given question as a function of the following variables:

- treatment factor (SuperBook versus paper)
- test factor (question difficulty)
- blocking factor (population)
- two-way interactions between these variables.

If the model fits adequately, terms are deleted to get a more parsimonious model.

Results. PROC CATMOD compared the subjects' scores on the easy questions to those of medium difficulty and also those of medium to hard difficulty. Overall, subjects did much better on the questions of medium difficulty than they did on the tough questions. Interestingly, the easy/paper question was difficult for the majority of subjects. Of the total frequency of 31, there were 15 possible response combinations. The treatment factor was significant ($p < .01$). The test factor was highly significant ($p < .001$). The blocking factor was not significant. The two-way interactions cannot be ignored; otherwise the model does not fit.

Conclusion

The results of this empirical study indicate that subjects performed better with SuperBook than they did with paper. The research team thus concluded that online access could substitute for the hard copy index. While these results were not surprising, it should be noted that the entire document set encompasses over 1500 pages and that the full complement of intended users would undoubtedly be less familiar with the contents of the memoranda. These two factors would seem to further enhance SuperBook's advantage over paper. As a client-server application, these policy documents would be generally available over a computer network, thereby facilitating their distribution and access to a much wider population.

In post-test, large-group discussions with the participants, the general agreement was that the agency should move to provide electronic access to its document collection. Following on the tradition of library automation projects, in which online public access catalogs have greatly improved the efficiency and productivity of information searches and subsequent access to particular items, new approaches to office records management may provide similar capabilities. As the cost-to-performance ratios of the necessary electronic records management systems continue to improve, they may lower transaction costs and bring unparalleled access to the vast array of public holdings.

Endnotes

1. SuperBook is a registered trademark of Bellcore.
2. Vast improvements in the technology in the two years since this study was undertaken would, we hope, lessen the resources that a similar study today would have to devote to these preparatory activities.
3. All the test subjects exhibited complete comfort with computers and seemed sufficiently adept at operating the SuperBook software after the orientation session. Furthermore, subjects were free to ask for any necessary technical assistance during the test session so that ability to use the software would not adversely affect ability to answer policy-related questions.

Chapter 10

USE OF BOOK REVIEWS BY SCHOLARS: IMPLICATIONS FOR ELECTRONIC PUBLISHING

Amanda Spink
University of North Texas

Linda Schamber
University of North Texas

Abstract

Although book reviews occupy considerable space in scholarly journals, very few previous studies have examined or provided detailed data on the utility or importance of book reviews to scholars. This chapter reports results from an initial study of science and technology scholars at the University of North Texas. The survey sought to determine (1) the importance and utility of book reviews for scholars' research and teaching, and (2) scholars' criteria for useful book reviews. Findings from this study hold implications for the contents of and access to electronic publications, and for further research.

This chapter begins with a brief overview of previous studies that sought to determine the importance of scholarly book reviews to the academic community. The research methodology for our study is then described, and this is accompanied in an appendix by a copy of the questionnaire used for the study. The results of our study and a brief analysis of the findings conclude the chapter.

Introduction

Studies examining scholars' use of printed materials is a necessary precursor to the development of electronic journals and the field of electronic publishing of scholarly research.[1] The promise of electronic publishing is of particular interest in scholarship, where timeliness and relevance of publications are crucial to the advancement of knowledge. The study reported in this chapter represents the initial phase of a larger study to determine the utility and viability of electronically published book reviews..

Related Studies

Scholarly book reviews historically have found interest primarily among three groups: scholars, publishers, and librarians. Book reviews allow scholars to keep abreast of new publications they may wish to acquire and provide a forum for peer review of theories and ideas. The writing of scholarly book reviews is also considered in the faculty promotion and tenure process. Yet almost no studies have examined the utility or importance of book reviews in the scholarly information seeking and research process.

The study's results will be important for the three groups cited previously. This information can assist publishers in determining the potential format, utility, and benefits of including book reviews in electronic scholarly journals. This study will also give librarians insights into the use of book reviews by scholars. Finally, the identification of useful criteria for book reviews gives publishers and scholars guidelines for improved writing and uses of book reviews.

Scholars

In a small German study, Huebner found scholarly book reviews ranked second only to direct recommendations by other scholars as the most important source of information on new books.[2] He also identified a ten-point list of criteria for a good book review. Diodato limited his investigation to the analysis of citations to arts and humanities book reviews.[3] He found scholarly cited book reviews infrequently and concluded they had little impact on scholarly research. The study discussed in this paper asked science and technology scholars to assess the utility of book reviews to research and teaching.

Book Publishers

Publishers use book reviews as a marketing tool to communicate information to librarians and scholars about their scholarly publications, by devoting many journal pages to book reviews. Many studies have investigated the characteristics of book reviews,[4,5] characteristics of reviewers,[6,7] and the proportion of books reviewed by scholarly journals.[8,9,10] Limited research has provided publishers with detailed data on the utility and importance of book reviews for scholars' research.

Librarians

The scholarly book review has generally served two purposes for librarians. First, as a current awareness tool providing information on new and forthcoming books; second, as an evaluation tool for the acquisition of books for the library collection. Many previous studies have examined the use of book reviews by librarians as book selection resources for acquisitions and collection development.[11-18]

Research Questions

The research questions investigated in this study were:

1. What sources do science and technology scholars use to obtain information about new books?
2. How do those scholars rate the importance of book reviews in their scholarly research and teaching?
3. What are science and technology scholars' criteria for useful book reviews?
4. What personal experience do science and technology scholars have with electronic media?

Research Methodology

Data was collected by surveying science and technology faculty members at the University of North Texas (UNT). Those individuals were surveyed as a convenient sample to test the methodology before proceeding to a larger sample. The survey questionnaire (Appendix A) was developed with a cover letter and distributed to 350 science and technology faculty members from the physics, computer science, mathematics, and engineering sciences departments. Fifty-three (15 percent) of the surveyed faculty members responded. The majority (69 percent) held the rank of assistant or associate professor out of a responding complement of two instructors, eighteen assistant professors, nineteen associate professors, nine full professors, four department chairs, and one dean. The number of male respondents was 47 (89 percent), roughly the same proportion as in the surveyed faculty overall.

Results

The results yielded data concerning scholars' behavior in seeking, evaluating, and using information about new books in their fields.

Sources of Book Reviews

Table 10.1 (page 118) shows the rank order of importance of sources for information on new books. The sources ranked first in importance by number of respondents were scholarly publications (26), followed by publishers catalogs or forthcoming booklists (17), and academic colleagues (6). This result does not concur with Huebner's finding of academic colleagues as the prime source of information on new books. Huebner's study was completed in Germany and his findings may reflect European scholars' approach to books. In our survey, the sources ranked second or lower in importance were newspapers, magazines, and library awareness services. Two-thirds, or 36 respondents, read one to five book reviews in the last month. Two respondents read six to ten book reviews; the remainder read none. A smaller group of ten respondents had written one to five book reviews in the past twelve months.

Importance of Book Reviews

Table 10.2 (page 119) shows the usefulness of scholarly book reviews to science and technology scholars' research and teaching. Respondents often suggested multiple reasons for reading book reviews, divided almost equally between research interests (34) and teaching interests (33), followed by general reading (19). Opinions on the usefulness of book reviews to research and teaching varied from "worthless" to "very useful." Those who rated reviews "very useful" or "useful" to their research (23) or teaching (28), barely outnumbered those who rated reviews of "limited value" or "worthless" to their research (22) or teaching (18). Science and technology scholars were divided on the usefulness of book reviews to their research and teaching.

Criteria for Useful Book Reviews

Table 10.3 (page 120) shows rank order of respondents' criteria for a useful book review. Rankings of the four criteria for evaluating the usefulness of a book review also varied widely. For many respondents, the criterion ranked highest (21 mentions) was a description of the contents of each chapter of a book. The reviewer's authority on the subject of the book was the next highest (11 mentions) to be chosen first even though that category was ranked third or fourth by about two-thirds of the respondents. Timeliness, or availability of the book review within six months of publication, was also ranked highest (9 mentions) by some respondents, but received nearly equal mentions for second and third places, and a few (4 mentions) as lowest in importance. Critical comments by reviewers were ranked highest by only four respondents.

Experience with Electronic Publications

Table 10.4 (page 121) shows the network services used by respondents. Although most respondents (85 percent) reported familiarity with the Internet, local networks, or various electronic services, few (28 percent) had read electronic journals. By far the most common use of electronic services was e-mail, used by 45 (85 percent) respondents. E-mail use was followed by library catalogs (39), electronic databases (27), bulletin boards (21), electronic journals

(15), computer conferences (9), and video conferences (2). Only eight respondents had read an electronic journal containing book reviews. However, 33 (62 percent) said they would be interested in electronic journals with book reviews.

Discussion

As electronic technologies lead scholars into a new era of publishing, it becomes necessary to reevaluate every component of current print publications to decide on the efficacy of conversion to electronic formats. This initial study investigated sources and uses of book reviews as an element of information among science and technology academics. The results suggest further research on users' criteria and expectations that may affect electronic publishing.

The transition to electronic publishing offers the opportunity to alter or improve journal content. Although respondents in this study indicate that usually they read book reviews for multiple reasons, their ratings of "usefulness" and their rankings of "criteria for evaluating usefulness" were highly inconsistent. Clearly further study of scholars' evaluations, including elicitation of additional criteria, would help shed light on the roles and importance of book reviews. Where scholars place a high value on reading descriptions of contents of new books, for example, simple tables of contents might be published immediately in advance of, or even in lieu of, critical reviews. The respondents also placed a relatively low value on "timeliness" of book reviews. This was not surprising as publishing electronically for the sake of immediacy may be unwarranted—science and technology books often contain information previously published in conference papers and journal articles.

Many other considerations enter the picture. The low value placed on timelines, for instance, may also reflect low expectations among scholars for a rapid turnaround as they are still relatively unfamiliar with electronic publishing. Nonetheless, the lag time between publication of a new book and its review may not be improved appreciably by electronic publishing because reviewers need as much time as ever to complete their reviews. Speedier production and distribution of electronic journals is only marginally helpful in that regard.

For publishers, the findings of this initial study suggest scholarly publications and publishers' information as the most likely sources for science and technology scholars seeking information on new books. The time seems right to conduct longitudinal studies of all aspects of scholarly publishing and communication as scholars' experience with electronic media increases.

Finally, sources of information are of major concern to librarians, who themselves are major users of book reviews. It is interesting that respondents ranked libraries last as sources of book reviews. Librarians might examine ways to expand access to book reviews, perhaps by offering resources they already use, directly from publishers or vendors.

Conclusions

The results of this initial study suggest sufficient interest among the scholars surveyed to justify pursuit of further research involving a larger and broader sample of respondents. In our case, additional research was conducted among humanities and social science scholars, including interviews about their use of book reviews.

REFERENCES

1. Landow, G. P. and P. Delany, eds., *The Digital Word: Text-Based Computing in the Humanities*. Cambridge, MA: The MIT Press, 1993.

2. Huebner, W. "On the Importance of Reviews Contained in Technical Journals for Information Dissemination," *Zentbl. Biblioth* 91. 1977: 216-220 (German: title translated).

3. Diodato, V. "Impact and Scholarliness in Arts and Humanities Book Reviews: A Citation Analysis," *Proceedings of the ASIS Annual Meeting,* 21. 1984: 217-221.

4. Bilhartz, T. D. "In 500 Words or Less: Academic Book Reviewing in American History,"*The History Teacher* 17. 1984: 525-536.

5. Stankus, T. "Looking for Tutors and Brokers: Comparing Expectations of Book and Journal Evaluators," *Library Trends.* Winter 1985: 349-365.

6. Buttlar, L. J. "Profiling Review Writers in the Library Periodical Literature," *RQ.* Winter 1990: 221-229.

7. Griffith, S. C. and M. A. Seipp, "Small Press Children's Books and Where to Find Them," *School Library Journal* 28. 1982: 28-32.

8. Macleod, B. "Library Journal and Choice: A Review of Reviewers," *Journal of Academic Librarianship* 7. 1981: 23-28.

9. Chen, C. C. *Biomedical, Scientific and Technical Book Reviewing.* Metuchen, NJ: Scarecrow Press, 1976.

10. Wiley, M. "How to Read a Book: Reflections on the Ethics of Book Reviewing," *Journal of Advanced Composition* 13. 1993: 477-492.

11. Blake, V. "The Role of Reviews and Reviewing Media in the Selection Process: An Examination of the Research Record," *Collection Management* 11. 1989: 1-40.

12. Futas, E. *Library Acquisition Policies and Procedures.* Phoenix, AR: Oryx Press, 1977.

13. Parker, J. M. "Scholarly Book Reviews in Literature Journals as Collection Development Sources for Librarians," *Collection Management* 11. 1989: 41-50.

14. Paul, S. K. and C. A. Nemeyer. "Book Marketing and Selection: Selected Findings From the Current AAP/ALA Study," *Publishers Weekly* 207. 1975: 42-45.

15. Serebnick, J. "Book Reviews and the Selection of Potentially Controversial Books in Public Libraries," *Library Quarterly* 51. 1981: 390-409.

16. ———. "An Analysis of Publishers of Books Reviewed in Key Library Journals," *Library and Information Science Research* 6. 1984: 289-303.

17. Shontz, D. and P. Hsu, "Book Reviews in Psychology and Related Fields," *Behavioral and Social Science Librarian* 8. 1989: 13-32.

18. Van Orden, P. "Promotion, Review and the Examination of Materials," *School Media Quarterly* 6. 1978: 120-132.

Table 10.1. Sources of Book Reviews—Science & Technology Scholars (No. Respondents = 53)

Sources	Ranking					
	1st	2nd	3rd	4th	5th	6th
Scholarly publications	26	5	7	2	1	1
Newspapers	0	4	4	3	8	4
Magazines	0	4	7	5	4	3
Publishers' information	17	12	10	3	1	0
Colleagues	6	18	6	5	3	0
Library services	0	3	0	6	2	8
Other	2	3	4	2	1	0
Subtotal	51	49	38	26	20	16
Missing Cases	2	4	15	27	33	37
Total	53	53	53	53	53	53

Table 10.2. Usefulness of Scholarly Reviews to Research and Teaching— Science & Technology Scholars (No. Respondents = 53)

Usefulness	Research		Teaching	
	Respondents	%	Respondents	%
Very useful	3	6%	4	8%
Useful	20	38%	24	45%
Neutral or indifferent	8	15%	5	9%
Limited value	10	19%	13	25%
Worthless	12	23%	5	9%
Subtotal	53	100%	51	96%
Missing Cases	0	0%	2	4%
Total	53	100%	53	100%

Table 10.3. Ranking of Respondents' Criteria for Useful Book Reviews—Science & Technology Scholars. (No. Respondents = 53)

Criteria	Rankings by number of respondents			
	1st	2nd	3rd	4th
Timeliness	9	7	9	4
Reviewer authority	11	6	15	18
Description of book contents	21	10	8	4
Critical comments	4	20	19	7
Subtotal	45	43	51	39
Missing cases	8	10	2	14
Total	53	53	53	53

Table 10.4. Network Services Used (No. Respondents = 53)

Network services	Respondents	%
Electronic mail	45	85%
Library catalogs	39	74%
Electronic databases	27	51%
Bulletin boards	21	4%
Electronic journals	15	28%
Computer conferences	9	17%
Video conferences	2	4%

APPENDIX

October 15th, 1994

Dear UNT Faculty Colleague,

I am seeking your assistance in the first pilot study phase of a major research project at the University of North Texas investigating various aspects of scholarly communication and the design of scholarly electronic science and technology publications.

The first phase of this research is a study investigating the use of book reviews in scholarly publications by science and technology scholars. Book reviews form a major component of scholarly publications. I would like to learn about your use of book reviews that appear in scholarly science and technology publications.

Your opinions are important-even if you don't read many book reviews. Please answer each question as completely as possible.

If you have any questions regarding the study or the survey, please don't hesitate to contact me at UNT extension 2187.

Many thanks for your assistance in this research project.

Amanda Spink, Ph.D.
Assistant Professor
Electronic Publishing Project

SURVEY ON THE ROLE OF BOOK REVIEWS ON SCIENCE AND TECHNOLOGY SCHOLARLY COMMUNICATION: IMPLICATIONS FOR ELECTRONIC PUBLISHING

The purpose of this survey is to learn more about the role of book reviews in the work of science and technology scholars. Your opinions are important—even if you don't read many book reviews. Please answer each question as completely as possible.

1. Do you <u>read book reviews</u> in scholarly journals? (Circle your response)

1 Yes 2 No

If your answer was **YES**, how many book reviews in scholarly journals have you <u>read</u> in the **LAST MONTH**? (Circle number of **SINGLE BEST** response)

 1 1-10 book reviews
 2 11-20 book reviews
 3 21-30 book reviews
 4 31-40 book reviews
 5 50+ book reviews

2. Do you read book reviews for any of the following **REASONS**? (Circle **YES** or **NO**)

 Research interests YES NO
 Teaching interests YES NO (Textbooks or class materials)
 General reading YES NO

3. How would you describe the **USEFULNESS TO YOUR RESEARCH** of scholarly book reviews? (Circle number of <u>SINGLE BEST</u> response)

 1 They are very useful
 2 They are useful
 3 I am neutral or indifferent to them
 4 They have limited value
 5 They are worthless

4. How <u>USEFUL</u> are scholarly book reviews in your selection of textbooks and reading materials for **TEACHING**? (Circle <u>SINGLE BEST</u> response)

 1 They are very useful
 2 They are useful
 3 I am neutral or indifferent to them
 4 They have limited value
 5 They are worthless

5. How many book reviews for scholarly publications have you **WRITTEN** in the last 12 months?

   _____

6. Are you a **BOOK REVIEW EDITOR** for a scholarly publication? If so, please name the publication

   _____

7. Please rank in <u>order of importance</u> the following sources you use for information on new books in science and technology.

   Book reviews in scholarly publications _____
   Book reviews in newspapers _____
   Book reviews in magazines _____
   Publishers forthcoming booklists or catalogs _____
   Academic colleagues _____
   Library awareness services _____
   Other sources _____

8. What is your PRIMARY SOURCE for information on <u>new books</u> in science and technology?

   _____

9. Please **RANK IN ORDER** of importance the following criteria for a <u>useful book review</u>.

   Timeliness of book review (available at the time
   of book publication or within six months) _____
   The book reviewer is an authority in the subject of the book _____
   Description of the contents of each chapter of the book _____
   Critical comments by reviewer on the quality of the book _____
   Other criteria (please specify) _____

   _____

ELECTRONIC JOURNALS AND BOOK REVIEWS

10. Do you use the Internet or other **electronic networks**? (Electronic networks are computers linked by telecommunications: linked workstations, dialup links—local, national or international). (Circle your response)

   1 Yes   2 No

126

If **YES**, which electronic networks do you use?

_____

_____

11. If you use electronic networks, which of the following **SERVICES** do you use?

Electronic mail (sending messages) _____

Electronic bulletin boards, mailing lists, discussion groups or computer conferencing systems _____

Videoconferencing _____

Electronic journals or newsletters _____

Electronic databases _____

Online library catalogs _____

12. If you have read any **ELECTRONIC JOURNALS OR NEWSLETTERS**, please name the journals or newsletters you have read?

_____

_____

13. If you have used an electronic journal or newsletter, were **BOOK REVIEWS** included? (Circle your response)

       1 Yes   2 No

14. Would you be **INTERESTED** in reading electronic journals or newsletters that provide electronic reviews of current books in science and technology? (Circle your response)

       1 Yes   2 No

IMPORTANT BACKGROUND INFORMATION

15. Gender (Circle number of your response)

    1 Male   2 Female

16. Academic status (Circle number of your response)

    1 Dean

    2 Chair of Department

    3 Full Professor

    4 Associate Professor

    5 Assistant Professor

    6 Instructor

    Other _____

17. Academic discipline (e.g., physics, math, chemistry)

CONCLUDING THE SURVEY

18. Is there anything further you would like to add regarding the role of book reviews of science and technology materials to your scholarly work?

19. Would you be interested in a short follow-up to this study, such as a brief telephone interview or in-person interview on specific aspects of your use of book reviews? (Circle your response)

        1 Yes   2 No

THANK YOU
Please return via UNT mail to:
Dr. Amanda Spink
Electronic Publishing Project SLIS
Information Sciences Building

SECTION THREE

THE COPYRIGHT CONTROVERSY

Chapter 11

COPYRIGHT ON THE INTERNET— WHAT'S AN AUTHOR TO DO?

Vicki L. Gregory
University of South Florida

W. Stanley Gregory
Thorington & Gregory

Abstract

Many authors and copyright holders are concerned about property rights for materials distributed in electronic form. They seek both to protect and to be compensated for the use of their intellectual properties. The situation calls for all information providers, whether working for a conventional brick-and-mortar library or within the amorphous walls of an electronic system, to examine the major issues with care. This chapter discusses these issues and highlights a few of the more promising solutions to the problems raised.[1]

The Copyright Problem

Clifford Stoll states the apparent problem this way:

> Without a massive change in copyright law . . . libraries can't put their collections online. It's not simply that copyright blocks bookless libraries. Rather, copyright is the solution to the more fundamental problem: we want to be paid for the use of our work—our intellectual property.[2]

What Stoll says is that we have something of a classic conundrum: adequate protection of authors' rights is impossible in the electronic environment (Stoll implies), which represents a black hole that will suck in all media sooner or later anyway. The corollary to this is either that we should not even try to protect authors—i.e., let all the world's materials go freely on line and damn the consequences; or we need in some way to change (and likely further complicate) existing copyright laws. Changing the copyright laws, we submit, will likely only increase the complication and broaden the confusion (an all-too-familiar consequence of legislative remedies generally).

We maintain to the contrary: the current copyright laws, in the United States at least, are basically adequate for their purpose and amenable to the requirements of authors. What is needed is both an adequate policing and enforcement mechanism and, more important, the will of both authors and those in control of information systems to implement it.

Certainly our view may not be revolutionary, but it is probably the minority opinion, if not anachronistic. Nicholas Negroponte offers the opposite view. He states that

> Copyright law is totally out of date. It is a Gutenberg artifact. Since it is a reactive process, it will probably have to break down completely before it is corrected.[3]

But what would Negroponte's correction be? He seems to imply that the whole idea of legal protection, and hence the encouragement of intellectual property development, is outmoded because enforcement depends on the print process itself. Nonetheless, copyright protection is certainly welcomed by the creators of intellectual property, as the volume of any recent year's filings with the copyright and trademark offices will attest. And it seems doubtful that the public policy goals underlying the law's provisions of protection for owners of intellectual property—i.e., the active development and dissemination to society at large of new thoughts, ideas, and processes—no longer remain valid. Without adequate protection of the right to reap appropriate financial rewards from the exercise of the mind, as well as those that may be earned by the sweat of the brow, advances in our philosophies, our machines, and our methods, would inevitably stall. If the only way for owners to ensure compensation for their creations is to hoard them and keep them secret, then far too many ideas would likely accompany their creators to the grave.

Copyright is essentially a governmental construct that, in American jurisprudence, traces from the English Parliament's 1710 enactment of what copyright experts refer to as the "Statute of Queen Anne." That law was the first explicit governmental recognition of the rights of authors respecting their works.[4] In the United States, copyright derives from no less an august source than the United States Constitution: among the other powers of Congress, the eighth clause of section 8, Article I, places the protection of authors and inventors on a par with the power to tax, to borrow, and to regulate commerce.

The wisdom of our eighteenth century founders that transfigured democratic philosophies into a form of government designed to attenuate the tendency toward extremes in human behavior may be hard to match among today's leaders, but now at least we can still form committees on matters of importance to us. On the matter at hand, for example, we have the National Information Infrastructure Task Force's Working Group on Intellectual Property. The "Executive Summary" of the Group's draft report presents (not necessarily in a style of prose as Olympian as one might wish) a confirmation of our somewhat conservative view:

> The Working Group concludes that, with the following limited amendments and clarifications, the Copyright Act will provide the necessary protection of rights in copyrighted works—and appropriate limitations on those rights.[5]

The changes in the area of copyright law recommended in the draft report are repeated in the later White Paper issued on September 5, 1995.[6] These "limited" changes include references to the electronic medium as well as books and phonorecords (as are mentioned in the 1976 Copyright Act). Changes are proposed to the copyright law as it relates to fair use (which has mainly been defined in academic situations as the *minimum* rights in the CONTU guidelines), distribution by transmission, publication, first sale and educational uses. The Working Group did note that "it is critical that researchers, students, and other members of the public have opportunities *online* equivalent to their current opportunities *off-line* to browse through copyrighted works in their schools and public libraries."[7]

The Working Group further makes a distinction between electronic transmission for the purpose of communication (and thereby fair use) and a transmission primarily for the purpose of distribution of the work (a privilege reserved for the copyright owner):

> The Working Group also recommends that the definition of "transmit" in Section 101 of the Copyright Act be amended to delineate between those transmissions that are communications of performances or displays and those that are distributions of reproductions.[8]

A very nice and fine distinction, indeed, but the Working Group gives little guidance in determining how one is to know the *purpose*, as opposed to the mere *content* of a transmission. In contrast to the rights of communication that it believes should be covered by fair use, the Working Group recommended that Section 106 of the Copyright Act be amended to reflect the reality that copies of works can be distributed to the public by electronic transmission and that such transmissions fall within the exclusive distribution rights of the copyright owner.

> The Working Group recommends that such a transmission be considered a distribution of a reproduction if the *primary purpose or effect* of the transmission is to distribute a *copy or phonorecord* of the work to the recipient of the transmission.[9]

In other words, copyright is not violated unless, of course, it is being violated— reasoning like that will get you an "F" in law school every time!

Another major issue with electronic copyright is that of the ease of copying electronic documents. Negroponte states that:

> Most people worry about copyright in terms of the ease of making copies. In the digital world, not only the ease is at issue, but also the fact that the digital copy is as perfect as the original and, with some fancy computing, even better. . . . [A] copy can be cleaned up, enhanced, and have noise removed. The copy is perfect.[10]

But is such a problem really all that new? Examples abound in many of the creative arts of original works enhanced by others: many musical compositions are often much improved when arranged and orchestrated by persons other than the composers of the original melodies. Although they may be the most apparent examples, rearrangements of the works of rock star tunesmiths are not the only instances of this phenomenon: Richard Rodgers, the great musical comedy composer, was, some say, only a competent if rather pedestrian arranger of his brilliant Broadway show tunes—much of what we perceive as the genius of his music reflects not just the original piano score but the improvements wrought upon it by the arranger and orchestrator.

As for the perfection of copies, the skilled art forger is far from a modern fraud; and we seem to have coexisted quite well for thirty or so years with essentially photographically accurate xerography (a patented process, and a trademarked name, by the way). Still, it would be unfair to say that the environment is not changing—the functional equivalent of xerography deliverable by the scanned electronic image and its easy, widespread dissemination is the real problem.

Negroponte further states that:

> When bits are bits, we have a whole new suite of questions, not just the old ones like piracy.
> The medium is no longer the message.[11]

Of course, protection from piracy is as old as the art. As a recent example, consider the copy machine "revolution" of the late 1960's. With a view toward ensuring that a photocopy was not mistaken for an original, many newly installed copiers in libraries (and most in law firms) were usually set up so as to underlay the copy with some sort of identifying mark, a watermark of sorts, to make it quite clear that the output was a copy and not the original. This practice has generally ceased, perhaps on the basis that few photocopies are really all that true to the original in "feel" (and in light of the copying process usually involving a slight—approximately 2 percent—increase in document image size). Still, it is interesting to note that IBM has recently announced an analogous process for indelibly watermarking electronic versions of documents digitally in order to denote the source of the information or the identity of the requester. Concomitant with this new technology are methods for accomplishing metering and billing for downloads.[12]

Fair Use from a Library and Higher Education Perspective

Librarians are generally concerned with maintaining the same rights for electronic publications that pertain to print media. The most important rights as identified by six library associations (The American Association of Law Libraries, the American Library Association, the Association of Academic Health Sciences Library Directors, the Association of Research Libraries, the Medical Library Association, and the Special Libraries Association) in a working document dated January 18, 1995, consist of the following:

- to read, listen to, or view copyrighted material privately, on site or remotely;
- to browse publicly marketed materials which are copyrighted;
- to experiment with variations of copyrighted materials for fair use, while preserving the integrity of the original;
- to make a first-generation copy (for personal use, scholarship, or research) of a copyrighted or library-owned work;
- to make transitory copies if ephemeral or incidental to a lawful use as long as they are retained only temporarily.[13]

That these concerns are shared by others in higher education is shown by the following statement of Samuel H. Smith, president of Washington State University and chair of the National Association of State Universities and Land Grant Colleges' Commission on Information Technologies:

Free inquiry and free expression are indispensable to the academic enterprise. Essential to the free exchange of ideas and dissemination of knowledge in higher education are preservation and continuation of these balance rights [i.e., fair use versus protection of intellectual property] in electronic as well as print environments.[14]

Thus, the doctrine of fair use must remain alive to accompany the protection provided to authors by copyright law, even though the electronic environment may make violation of fair use principles more difficult to detect and monitor.

Fair Use from a Legal Perspective

The copyright laws of the United States intend that the holder of a copyright should enjoy a considerable number of exclusive legal rights—including the right to reproduce his or her own work. Nonetheless, the fair use doctrine, which must be seen as invasive of the author's exclusive rights, is not construed in the narrow way the law typically reserves for special exceptions to general statutory rules. This anomaly occurs partly because copyright law generally is based not on case law (sometimes confused with the common law) but rather upon a statutory underpinning. Fair use, however, is a judicial concept, that has, in the Copyright Act of 1976,[15] worked its way into the statute books.

We are fortunate that the jurisprudence enveloping the fair use doctrine of copyright law is not quite so amorphous as the fog surrounding that hero of the common law, the "reasonable man." Most courts of law in this country try to follow the precept that what a reasonable human would have done in a particular circumstance is what you should have done. The problem is you find out only later, and then only from a court of law after much legal wrangling and expense. The statutory enshrinement of the judicial doctrine of fair use does make this a bit easier—Congress in Section 107 of the Copyright Act of 1976 has (kind of) told us what fair use actually is, by defining what something else, i.e., infringement, is not:

> [F]air use of a copyrighted work . . . for purposes such as criticism, comment, news reporting, teaching . . . scholarship, or research is not an infringement of copyright.

Unfortunately, this doesn't take us very far. The first rule of statutory construction ("read on") obviously applies here, and Congress has given us several guidelines to live by, which are remarkably flexible and applicable to the electronic environment:

> In determining whether the use made of a work in any particular case is a fair use the factors to be considered shall include—(1) the purpose and character of the use, including whether such use is of a commercial nature or is for nonprofit educational purposes; (2)

the nature of the copyrighted work; (3) the amount and substantiality of the portion used in relation to the copyrighted work as a whole; and (4) the effect of the use upon the potential market for or value of the copyrighted work.[16]

These four factors, however, fail to give information providers the kind of bright line guidance that they, and their legal advisors, would like to receive. Not one of the factors in itself is binding on the conclusion of whether a use is fair: the wisdom of the law in this respect is evident. It is intentionally designed as a flexible standard rather than an ironclad rule to be slavishly applied.

To a very considerable degree, then, each case coming before a court stands or falls on its individual merits. Perhaps this characteristic of determining the proper application of the fair use concept to the electronic environment's numberless transactions gives information providers pause. And it suggests that just throwing one's hands up may be the appropriate response—letting the Internet stay fully wild, woolly and free, if not necessarily the right thing to do, might seem the only economically practical alternative.

But the idea of applying general principles on a case-by-case basis as a method of developing a cogent body of law is certainly not new; therefore, why should this concept prove anymore difficult to apply to the cyberspace environment than to any other field of human endeavor? The Copyright Act in no way indicates that its fair use limitations are restricted to the print environment. The statutory factors may need examination and interpretation by the courts in the context of the new technologies, but if the law makes any sense in terms of its application in the print world, it certainly must remain credible in the electronic environment.

Ah, but it is said that the copyright laws are now so easily violated—and in a big-time way—that we could scan in the *Encyclopaedia Britannica* and post it at the friendly neighborhood Web site. Well, maybe not with absolute ease and rather a long way from absolute fidelity to the original, but certainly analogous activities are conducted every single day. For examples, contemplate the software copying problem in light of activities routinely practiced in any computer-literate household that has more than one processor, or consider the software piracy apparently rampant in many developing nations.

But the routine breaking of the copyright laws by otherwise law-abiding citizens does not make a compelling argument for new legislation. Legalizing everything in order to eliminate crime is an old joke that is really at the heart of the argument that, since the Web makes violation of the laws easier, we should change the laws to comport with what the violators are doing.

Proposed Solutions to the Fair Use
Dilemma in the Electronic Environment

If, then, the conceptual underpinnings of current copyright protection are sound, the problem devolves to one of enforcement, policing, and document security. In essence, the solution calls for the will and resources to ensure that the purposes of the copyright law are both respected and carried out. Librarians may be as ill-equipped to police electronic fair use of materials as are college football coaches to prevent their young stars from taking money from unscrupulous sports agents or alumni—but that excuses neither group from their responsibilities as overseers. Both groups must set the example by not ignoring the problem but behaving proactively.

Information providers can ameliorate most of the problems of "unfair use" through the securing of site licenses and working with the Copyright Clearance Center. This is so because most of the *in terrorem* examples of the difficulties in applying existing copyright laws to the electronic sphere that are cited to justify a "wild and free" Internet involve essentially the absurd and undoubtedly isolated event, such as the scanned-in encyclopedia. In the real world it is difficult to conceive of anyone taking the time to do something like that except in anticipation of substantial financial gain, which could not accrue without leaving clear tracks straight to the perpetrator. And how many rational people would buy the electronic bootlegger's product with confidence in its accuracy and completeness, which the legitimate holder of the product's copyright can reasonably be expected to ensure? Surely there will always exist a market for second-rate knockoffs of original goods (even prescription pharmaceuticals these days), but those portions of the market, in the final analysis, simply do not constitute a clear and significant justification for major change in the laws—whether dealing with tangible or intellectual property.

Who Should Hold the Copyright on Scholarly Works?

If enforcement of copyright can be said to begin at home, the question of who should hold the copyright on scholarly works has great implications for the advancement of knowledge in the electronic information age. For example, when an author has signed over the copyright for his/her work to the publisher of a scholarly journal, as is the standard practice, can the author then legally send an electronic copy of that work to a colleague over the Internet? For the advancement of knowledge (and "to promote the progress of science and useful arts"[17]), shouldn't the author be legally entitled to do so? Walt Crawford and Michael Gorman offer the simplest and doubtless the most satisfactory solution to this dilemma:

Scholars should protect their copyrights. Assignment of copyrights is not general practice in magazine and trade book publishing, and should not be considered standard practice for scholarly publishing.[18]

Although new authors may find it difficult, established authors can and do often insist on retaining the copyrights on their articles. If scholars as a whole became more concerned about the issue of retaining copyright, more journals might as a matter of policy allow authors at least the option of retaining the copyrights on their submissions.

According to Laura Gasaway, authors' assigning copyrights to publishers of scholarly journals was not a problem until about twenty years ago. Until that time, scholarly journals were generally published by scholarly societies that did not require authors to relinquish full copyrights.

Scholarly societies had little interest in taking the entire copyright from the author since their primary emphasis in publishing journals was the distribution of research data for and to their members. Thus, faculty were free to reuse their works later as book chapters, to update articles for republication, to reproduce them for distribution to the faculty member's own classes, and to make copies available to their colleagues upon request.[19]

As more and more scholarly journals came to be published by commercial publishers, the reasons for publication turned from pure scholarly interest to that of a for-profit business. Gasaway notes:

Against this backdrop, it is natural to consider alternative publication and distribution methods, especially since academic authors currently receive little or no compensation for assigning their rights in an article to a publisher. . . . University libraries are faced with repurchasing the scholarly articles of their own faculty members, often at greatly inflated prices. . . . Thus, academic institutions are reexamining the current situation and considering whether universities themselves might become publishers by offering the scholarly contributions of their faculty authors electronically in a networked environment.[20]

Another trend that has great merit is for authors to indicate within the work itself what is acceptable or fair use of that electronic document by others. By so doing, an author might avoid the placing of one's rights in the tender mercies of a court of law. Many items available via the Internet now contain authors' statements such as "may be used for educational/scholarly purposes [or more general usage] as long as the document is transmitted in its entirety and contains this copyright notice." Sometimes authors will specify just the use of the copyright statement as being sufficient, and the transmittal of the entire document is not required.

Continuing Importance of Copyright

The underlying motivation of the copyright principle has never been to enrich authors, no matter how deserving, but rather to ensure that information, ideas, processes, etc. are actually disseminated to the public, and not squirreled away in a basement or attic. Barbara Ringer, while serving as U.S. Register of Copyrights, wrote:

> If the users of the new communications technologies insist on using authors' works without giving some appropriate compensation in return, they will find that sooner or later there will be no authors worth reading and no works worth reproducing.[21]

In other words, given the current publishing environment and continued importance of the protections afforded authors by the copyright law, if all the electronic materials available on the Internet are made available for free use with no restrictions, that is to say, if the copyright laws are allowed to wither away through inactive enforcement, the net will eventually, if it is not already, be dominated by valueless material, making the true gems of knowledge difficult or impossible to find on it because of the eventual consequent unwillingness of publishers and authors to allow any electronic use at all of their materials.

Endnotes

1. For an excellent general overview, see Janis H. Bruwelheide, *The Copyright Primer for Librarians and Educators*. Chicago and London: American Library Association. 1995.

2. Stoll, Clifford. *Silicon Snake Oil: Second Thoughts on the Information Highway*. New York: Doubleday. 1995. p. 178.

3. Negroponte, Nicholas: *Being Digital*. New York: Knopf. 1995. p. 58.

4. Bielefield, Arlene, and Lawrence Cheeseman. *Libraries and Copyright Law*. New York and London: Neal-Schuman Publishers, Inc. 1993. pp. 26-27.

5. Executive Summary reprinted in full in the *Bulletin of the American Society for Information Science* 20 (August-September 1994): 2-4. Quoted material on page 2. The complete report is available at the following URL: http://www.uspto. gov/niip.html

6. *Intellectual Property and the National Information Infrastructure: Executive Summary.* September 5, 1995. URL: http://www. uspto.gov/web/ipnii/execsum.html

7. Ibid., p. 3.

8. Ibid., p. 2.

9. Ibid., p. 2.

10. Negroponte. *Being Digital*, p. 58.

11. Ibid., p. 61.

12. Lunin, Lois F. "IBM Announces Electronic Copyright Solutions." *Information Today* 12 (May 1995). pp. 1, 3.

13. *Fair Use in the Electronic Age: Serving the Public Interest.* Working document dated January 18, 1995, pp. 6-7. URL: http://arl.cni.org/scomm/copyright/uses.html

14. Smith, Samuel H. "Partnerships: Keys to the Future of Information Technology." *NASULGC Newsline* 4 (September 1995). p. 7.

15. Title 17, United States Code.

16. Title 17, United States Code §107.

17. U.S. Constitution, art. I, sec. 8, clause 8.

18. Crawford, Walt, and Michael Gorman. *Future Libraries: Dreams, Madness, & Reality.* Chicago: American Library Association, 1995. p. 164.

19. Gasaway, Laura N. "Scholarly Publication and Copyright in Networked Electronic Publishing." *Library Trends* 13 (1995). p. 680.

20. Ibid., p. 681.

21. Ringer, Barbara. "Copyright and the Future of Authorship." Reprinted in *Library Journal* 119 (November 15, 1994: S2-3. Originally published in *Library Journal* in the issue dated January 1, 1976.

Index

academic publishing on the Internet, 82, 83-84

AgNIC. *See* Agricultural Network Information Center

Agricultural Communicators in Education, 100

agricultural information system, 95-104

    benefits of, 103-104

    cost of, 102-103

    features of, 98-102

    proposal for, 95-98

Agricultural Network Alliance (ANA), 95

Agricultural Network Information Center (AgNIC), 95, 101

AHIP. *See* Getty Art History Information Program

American Association of Law Libraries, The, 135

American Library Association, 42, 135

American Society for Horticultural Science (ASHS), 96-97, 100, 101

American Society for Information Science (ASIS), 4, 100, 103

ANA. *See* Agricultural Network Alliance

Art History Information Program (AHIP). *See* Getty Art History Information Program

ASHS. *See* American Society for Horticultural Science

ASIS. *See* American Society for Information Science

Association of Academic Health Sciences Library Directors, 135

Association of Research Libraries, 135

Atkins, Daniel E., 99

Atlantic Canada Organization for Research Networking, 76

Atlantic Television System, 67, 76

Australian Bibliographic Network, 43

authors, concerns of in electronic publishing, 131-132

Baton Broadcasting, Inc., 76
Bellcore Laboratories, 108
Berkeley Finding Aid Project (BFAP). *See* Encoded Archival
    Description (EAD)
book reviews, importance of, 113-118
    research project for, 115-118, *120-123*
    to librarians, 114-115, 117-118
    to publishers, 114, 117
    to scholars, 113, 114-115, 117-118
Brown University
    Campus Wide Information System (CWIS), 81, 85-88, 93
    World Wide Web (WWW) system, 81, 88-89, 93

California Institute of Technology, 99
Campus Wide Information System (CWIS). *See* Brown University
Canadian Heritage Information Network, 13
Canadian Museum of Civilivation, 13
Carnegie Mellon University Lycos project, 45
cataloging and catalogs, 41-52
    electronic, 41, 43-52
    Internet indexes, 45-48
    traditional, 42-43
Categories for the Description of Works of Art, 20, 23
centralization/decentralization in organizations, 84-85, 89-90
Chicago Tribune, 70
CHIN. *See* Canadian Heritage Information Network
Chinese text. *See* encoding of Chinese text
CHIO. *See* Cultural Heritage Information Online
Chronicle-Health, The, 76
CIDOC (Internationl Council of Museums), 16
CIMI. *See* Consortium for the Computer Interchange of Museum
    Information
Clarinet online news service, 86
CND-Chinese Magazine, 60, 62-63, 64
Coalition for Networked Information (CNI), 13, 95
College Art Association (CAA), 23
college electronic publishing. *see* university electronic publishing
Communication Technology and Distance Education (CTDE), *102*
Computer Technology Research (CTR), 103, 104
Consortium for the Computer Interchange of Museum Information
    (CIMI), 9, 12-23
    link naming mechanism, 21-22

model for integrating cultural heritage information, 14-17
purpose of, 9
SGML Document Type Definition (DTD), 17-21
Content Standards for Digital Geospatial Metadata, 32
Constitution. *See* United States Constitution
Cooperative State Research, Education and Extension Service.
    See United States Department of Agriculture copyright, 131-140
    and fair use concerns, 135-138
    continuing importance of, 140
    of scholarly works, 138-140
    problems for electronic publishing, 131-135
Copyright Act of 1976, 133-134, 136, 137
Copyright Clearance Center, 138
Corbis, 13
Cornell University Mann Library, 100
Courtauld Institute. *See* Witt Library
CSREES. *See* United States Department of Agriculture
CTR. *See* Computer Technology Research
cultural heritage information
    archives of, 9-10
    authorities, 15-16
    CIMI model, 14-17
    digitization of, 11, *12*
    in museums, 9-11
    multimedia for, 13
    on the Internet, 13, 14, 22
    points of view, 16-17
    sources of, 9, 15
    standards for, 11-12
Cultural Heritage Information Online (CHIO), 13-14, 16, 17, 22

Dalhousie University, 76
Delorme, Inc., 30
Department of Agriculture (U.S.). *See* United States Department of
    Agriculture
Department of Commerce (U.S.). *See* National Telecommunications and
    Information Administration
Digital Equipment Corp., 108
Dow Jones, 70

Eastman Kodak Company, 13
electronic news, 67-79

advertisements in, 74-75
as a digital library, 67-69, 70-74
differences from newspaper databases, 69
prototypes for, 76-79
technical requirements, 75
electronic publishing
and organizational structure, 81, 89-90
background to, 1
copyright problems, 131-140
in colleges and universities, 81-83, 84-93
issues in, 1-4
of agricultural information, 95-104
of Chinese text, 56-63
of journals, 113
of news, 67-79
of scholarly research, 113
on the Internet, 55-56
vs. paper-based versions, 107-111
Encoded Archival Description (EAD), 23
encoding of Chinese text, 57-63
Engineering Electronic Library (EELS), 45, 46
English Parliment, 132

fair use, 135-138
Federal Geographic Data Committee, 27, 29, 30, 32
Federal Information Processing Standards (FIPS)
FIPS 173, 33, 37. (*See also* Spatial Data Transfer Standard)
FIPS 192, 35
FGDC. *See* Federal Geographic Data Committee
formal public identifiers (FPI), 21-22
FPI. *see* formal public identifiers

Geographic Information Systems (GIS), 28
geospatial information on the Internet, 30, 32, 35, 38
Getty Art History Information Program, 13
GILS. *See* Government Information Locator Service
Gingrich, Newt, 3
GIS. *See* Geographic Information Systems
GISDS. *See* Global Information System for Decision Support
Global Information System for Decision Support (GISDS) (*see also*
agricultural information system; United States Department of
Agriculture)

HortBase pilot program, 96-97
    query systems for, 101
    support for, 101-102
government documents, access to, 107-111
Government Information Locator Service (GILS), 27, 29, 33
Green, James, 96

Halifax Herald Limited, The, 67, 76
HortBase, 95-104
    authors/reviewers of, 98
    description of, 95-96
    developers of, 97
    files for, *96*, 98-101
HTML. *See* hypertext markup language
HTTP. *See* hypertext transfer protocol
Hua Xia Wen Zai (HXWZ). See *CND-Chinese Magazine*
Huebner, W., 114, 116
hypertext markup language (HTML), 22, 49, 50
hypertext transfer protocol (http), 21

indexing projects on the Internet, 45-49
Information Interchange Model, 70
International Council of Museums Documentation Committee, 16, 23
International Standard Book Number (ISBN), 21
Internet
    academic publishing on, 83-84
    access, 2, 4
    cultural heritage information, 13, 14, 22
    geospatial information, 28, 30, 33, 36
    indexing projects, 45-49
    library catalogs, 43-52
    use by librarians, 99-100
Internet Engineering Task Force, 103
Internet Public Library, 4
ISBN. *See* International Standard Book Number
ISO 2709 (MARC), 13. (*See also* USMARC format)
ISO 8879, 13. (*See also* Standard Generalized Markup Language)

Kodak. *See* Eastman Kodak Company

Lewis, Nathan, 99
librarians
    importance of book reviews to, 114-115, 117-118

    role in electronic publishing, 4
    use of the Internet, 99-100
libraries, and fair use concerns, 135-136
libraries, future of, 4, 41-42
library catalogs on the Internet, 43-52
Library of Congress, 43
link naming mechanism, 21-22
Lund University Library, 45
Lycos. *See* Carnegie Mellon University

Maritime Telephone & Telegraph, 78
MCN. *See* Museum Computer Network
Mead Data Center, 70
Medical Library Association, 135
Miami Herald, 70
Montana, State of, 30, 32
multimedia
    definition of, 103-104
    for cultural heritage information, 13
    for electronic news, 67
    for horticultural information, 97
    growth of, 104
    issues in, 1, 3
Multimedia Toolbook, 76
Museum Computer Network (MCN), 12, 13, 23
Museum Documentation Association (MDA), 13
Museum Informatics Project (Univ. of California at Berkeley), 13
museums' cultural heritage information, 9-11

National Agricultural Library (NAL). *See* United States Department of
    Agriculture
National Association of State Universities and Land Grant Colleges'
    Commission on Information Technologies, 135
National Endowment for the Humanities (NEH), 13
National Gallery of Art (NGA), 13
National Geospatial Data Clearinghouse, 27, 30
National Information Infrastructure, 33, 35, 133-134
National Institute for Standards and Technology (NIST), 35
National Museum of American Art (NMAA), 13
National Spatial Data Infrastructure (NSDI), 32
National Technical Library of Denmark, The, 45

National Telecommunications and Information Administration (NTIA), 13
NEH. *See*: National Endowment for the Humanties
NetFirst. *See* OCLC
networks (electronic) (*See also* Internet)
for delivering news, 69, 70
for information, 1
technical requirements for news delivery, 75-76
New York Times, The, 70
newspaper databases, 69
NGDC. *See* National Geographic Data Clearinghouse
NIST. *See* National Institute for Standards and Technology
NMAA. *See* National Museum of American Art
Nordic WAIS/World Wide Web Project, 45-46
NORDINFO, 45
NSDI. *See* National Spatial Data Infrastructure
NTIA. *See* National Telecommunications and Information Administraion

OCLC, 43
Cataloging Internet Project, 47
Internet Cataloging Resources Project, 47
NetFirst, 45
Office of Manpower and Budget (OMB), 29, 35
online public access catalogs, 111
Oregon State University Department of Horticulture, 98
Oregon State University Kerr Library, 100

Panorama conversion software. *See* SoftQuad
Parliament (Great Britain). *See* English Parliament
Philadelphia Museum of Art, 13
property rights. *see* copyright
publishers, importance of book reviews to, 114, 117
Purdue University library, 100

RAMA. *See* Remote Access to Museum Archives
Remote Access to Museum Archives (RAMA), 13
Research Libraries Group (RLG), The, 13
RLG. *See* Research Libraries Group, The
RLIN, 43

scholars, importance of book reviews to, 113, 114-115, 117
Science Education and Resource Development (SERD), *102*

SDTS. *See* Spatial Data Transfer Standard
SGML. *See* Standard Generalized Markup Language
SoftQuad, 22
Spatial Data Transfer Standard (SDTS), 33, 36, 37
spatial information, 27-38
    barriers to access, 28-32
    federal programs, 32-38
Special Libraries Association, 135
Standard Generalized Markup Language (SGML), 13
    Document Type Definition (DTD), 14
    for encoding attributes, 19
    Universal Text Format (UTF), 70
standards (*See also* Standard Generalized Markup Language)
    for agricultural data, 95, 96
    for bibliographic data, 50
    for cartographic and spatial information products, 27, 32-38
    for cultural heritage information, 11-12
    for electronic formats, 2, 89, 92, 103
Stanford University "Yahoo" system, 45
State University of New York (SUNY), 108, 109
State University of New York at Albany, Center for Technology in
    Government (CTG), 107, 108
Statute of Queen Anne, 132
Sun Microsystems, 76-77
SuperBook Project, 108-111
Swedish University of Technology Libraries, 45, 46

Topological Vector Profile (TVP), 37
TVP. *See* Topological Vector Profile

Uniform Resource Locator (URL)
    addresses, 43, 47, 49, 50, 51
    function of, 21
    indexing of, 45
United States Constitution, 132
United States Department of Agriculture
    Agricultural Experiment Stations, National Research Initiatives, 101
    Cooperative State Research, Education and Extension Service
        (CSREES), 95
    CSREES Global Information System for Decision Support
        (GISDS), 96, 97, 104
    Extension Service, 97

National Agricultural Library, 97
United States Geological Survey (USGS), 27, 29
Universal Bi-directional Interactive Consortium, 104
Universal Text Format (UTF). *See* Standard Generalized Markup
    Language
university electronic publishing, 81-93
University of California at Berkeley, 100. (*See also* Museum Informatics
        Project)
University of California Division of Library Automation, 13
University of London. *See*: Warburg Institute
University of Michigan School of Information and Library Studies, 99
University of North Texas, 113, 115
University of Virginia Library project, 47, 49
URL. *See* Uniform Resource Locator
USDA-CSREES. *See* United States Department of Agriculture
USGS. *See* United States Geological Survey
USMARC format, 11, 20
    Archival and Manuscripts Control (USMARC AMC), 12

Vector Product Format (VPF), 33, 37
Victoria & Albert Museum, 13
VPF. *See* Vector Product Format

Warburg Institute, 9, 11
Washington State University, 135
Witt Library, 10, 11
World Wide Web (*See also* Internet)
    at Brown University, 81, 88-89, 93
    browsers, 22
    Nordic WAIS/World Wide Web Project, 45-46
    OCLC NetFirst system, 46
    sites for museums' digital files, 11
    use of hypertext transfer protocol (HTTP) on, 21

Z39.50 protocol, 13, 33, 35